The PRINCIPLE of INTERCHANGE
~
and Other Stories

~ P.V. LeForge ~

The PRINCIPLE of INTERCHANGE
and Other Stories

~ P.V. LeForge ~

Paperback Rack Books
Tallahassee, Anchorage

A PAPERBACK RACK BOOKS PUBLICATION

"Railroad Days," "Action," and "Metamorphosis of an Elvis Presley Impersonator" first appeared in *Sun Dog: The Southwest Review.* "The Principle of Interchange" first appeared in *Cache Review.* "Abe Mott" was first published in *The Wisconsin Review.* "Souls" made its first appearance in *The Northern New England Review.* The author is grateful to these and all other small press magazines for the pat on the back that is a writer's highest, and sometimes only, reward.

Library of Congress Catalog Card Number: 89-92412

ISBN 0-9624878-0-5

Manufactured in the United States of America

First Edition: April, 1990

10 9 8 7 6 5 4 3 2 1

For P. F. Sloan and Janis Ian
(who inspired my early efforts with their own)

Contents

Introduction

I like to tell stories. Fish tales, sob stories, sports anecdotes, family secrets—you name it and I probably have a barrelful. But telling stories at gatherings or over dinner is one thing; writing them down is quite another. No longer is it okay to dredge up conveniently pertinent memories of an old friendship for the purpose of putting something in perspective or simply to make people laugh. On paper, it has to be a *story*. There have to be characters who talk a certain way and have views and ideas on a variety of subjects; situations must be plausible; the theme should be subtle but perceivable; and someone must be able to *learn* something from the mess.

This is difficult if the author doesn't have total control over a story's characters, and I never do. In fact, I often feel that my characters control me, or at least help me out when I go off in a wrong direction. They're patient and whimsical, sometimes allowing me to follow my outline for several pages before bumping me back on the right path. "Hold on there, Jack," they say. "Save yourself some grief and let us show you how we'd really act in this situation."

So I let them; and they tell me their own stories. Occasionally I hear the rantings of a near maniac, but just as often I spot a quirk or feel a sensitivity that I had not previously recognized. Sometimes I assimilate these stories and put them into my own words; more often I let the characters speak for themselves. So if storytelling is in my blood, it's also in the blood of my characters. And my characters are not only within me, they're somewhere outside of me as well.

But if these storybook people exist on some level of the collective unconscious, the situations in which they find themselves are either made up or situations I've found myself in at one time or another. I suppose that there are almost as many reasons for writing as there are writers, but surely one of the most common is to try to comprehend why people you know act the way they do. Just as readers wonder how they themselves would act in out-of-the-ordinary circumstances.

I'm not sure where my themes come from. I recently looked over a few dozen contemporary short story collections and was generally impressed with the overall talent of the authors and the continuity between one story and the next. Still, it was a little disturbing to read many of the same stories over and over again—not only within single collections by one author, but over several different collections by different authors. Like, where's the party and how can we get totally wasted? I'm into ennui as much as the next person, but I'm not sure that despair should be chic. In *this* collection, only "Muffy" wallows.

Some of these stories, especially "Vandals" and "Railroad Days," recall my childhood, when I alternated afternoons playing baseball and singing in a church choir. Others, such as "Abe Mott," 'Silk and Other Fine Things," and "Souls," spring from my interest in other cultures.

But if there's a real theme tying these stories together, it has to do with a secret project of mine (both in this life and probably the next ten): convincing people to like and respect each other. Not the easiest thing to do in practice, but a piece of cake to fit into a story. This humanism is something that has protected my thin skin through the hailstorms and snow flurries of the political climate over the last couple of decades. "In Canton" and "The Principle of Interchange" work from a feministic angle. "The Man Who Wrote Letters to Comic Books" and, in a grotesque way, "The Sexless Ones," treat the socially and culturally displaced. "Killing the Assassin" is my anti-death-penalty story, and "The Bowl of Sunshine" comes at it from a magical perspective. They all try.

In reviewing these stories for collective publication, I find that I have learned from each of them something about myself. I hope a thought or two gets through to everyone who reads them. If so, the principle of interchange will have been invoked: the reader will carry away from the bookstore something fresh; not only the book, but the characters, thoughts, and ideas that people it. At the same time, perhaps reading the book might cause something to be sloughed off—prejudices, old values, boredom.

Publishing a collection that was years in the writing is like having a retrospective. It's a good feeling. Like the paintings of a visual artist, stories are often likened to children. I feel that way, too, but I also feel that after a certain number of years, it is time to get the children out of the house so that I can get on with the rest of my life.

Lately, I've been working on novels—blustery and mysterious affairs—with blowhards, wimps, and other fine people vying for attention over dozens of chapters. But experiencing these clashes as they are created on the page makes me realize that a novel is little more than a long story made up of a lot of shorter stories. My characters still talk to me, but there are more of them now, and they all tend to speak at the same time.

If I'm disciplined enough to write another book of stories—and lucky enough to have another retrospective twenty years from now—I hope I will have avoided many of the mistakes I have made here. I hope also that my characters will still be stretching their imaginations, rattling off their good yarns, and, ultimately, making their own myths.

I don't know what I could do to stop them.

PVL
Tallahassee
January, 1990

Vandals

The church of Santa Teresa de las Carnaciones stood behind crenelated walls on the eastern edge of the Old Section of Rinconada. The Old Section itself was mostly deserted now, the huge, three-story houses empty and boarded up. But it was grand nonetheless. The streets were paved with smooth stones, and the houses were surrounded by trellised iron fences wrought in the high style of the rich dons. But the dons were long gone, and with them their traditions. High grass and weeds encroached into the porches and grew through the trellises.

The boy turned toward Santa Teresa. The church, its paint sun-baked into a tired gray, was flanked by a bell tower on the right and a cloister on the left. The three parts were connected through the transepts. The bell tower of the church was very tall and could be seen from almost every house in the Old Section. In front of the church was a spacious lawn with several blossoming mimosa trees, freshly trimmed. Behind it, Miguel caught the murmur of the sea.

Miguel passed through the high iron gate and entered the grounds. He had been told to walk to the left of the chapel, to the long low building that used to serve as cloisters for monks. A high wooden door closed off the building from the outside. The imposing door made Miguel feel insignificant. Had the General once entered this very door? Miguel lifted a heavy brass ring and pounded out a faintly echoing tattoo. Behind him, the bell tower threw a giant shadow across the lawn.

The door opened halfway without a sound, and a boy Miguel's age or a little older peered out at him. The boy was taller than Miguel, gaunt and red-lipped. He was dressed in dark blue choir robes.

"What do you want?" asked the boy.

"I wish to speak to Señor Ramos," said Miguel.

"Señor Ramos sees no one at this time of day."

"But isn't he the choirmaster?"

"Yes, but the choirmaster is busy."

Miguel knew that the boy was lying. He too would have lied in the boy's place. In Manzanillo it had been Miguel who would look out the door while others asked questions. There, Miguel had been a monitor in the choir. He found that he could lose little by lying and gain much. He had been trusted to keep the younger members of the choir in line. He had also bullied them and made them run errands for him. Sometimes a penitent sinner would come to the wrong door and Miguel or one of this friends would ask him or her to make an offering. With the money they would buy sodas and cigarettes. The bullying and the tricks had always gone on. Once, Miguel himself had been bullied. It was traditional, and Miguel would no more have thought of altering it than he would have thought of changing the liturgy.

And he had learned to make his responses quickly. "I was told by my employer to see Señor Ramos right away," he said.

"Tell me your business and I will relay it to the choirmaster when I can."

"I have a cartload of votive candles around the other side. Ask him where he wishes me to put them."

"You have candles?"

"Yes, a dozen new boxes."

"I know where they go. Show me where they are and I will unload them."

Miguel was perturbed that the boy in robes thought him so stupid. Had there really been candles, Miguel knew that the gaunt boy would have hidden some in the bushes to sell later. He would then have reported to the choirmaster that all were accounted for. For the work he did, the choirmaster would probably have rewarded him as well. As it was, there were no candles, and when the boy came out of the room and moved beyond Miguel's pointing finger, Miguel stepped quickly through the opening and bolted the door behind him.

He was in a high-ceilinged antechamber. Across the room, a row of dim lights revealed a hallway leading to rooms where

monks once lived and slept. Thick beams crisscrossed over
Miguel's head. There were no chairs, tables, or ornaments of
any kind. Only the high, arched doorway and the imposing height
of the room gave any indication that he was in a church.

"Hey kid, what are you doing? Let me in!"

Miguel ignored him. He heard the tinkling of single notes on
a piano. The notes came from one of the rooms off the corridor.

"I'm not supposed to wear my robes outside. Open before the
Padre sees." Miguel listened as the boy began pounding on the
door—softly and cautiously at first, then a bit louder. The door
was thick and high, and the dull pounding echoed faintly in the
empty room. The noise attracted a small boy of ten or so from
one of the rooms near the tinkling piano. He, too, wore the deep
blue robes of a choirboy.

"What is Catalano doing outside?" asked the boy.

"I don't know. Which is the choirmaster's room?"

"There: the last one on the right."

"He is alone?"

"Yes. Shall I let Catalano back in?"

"If you want."

"He may give me a beating."

"Don't, then."

Miguel walked down the corridor. The choirmaster's door was
open and Miguel saw him sitting at a piano, writing musical symbols in a notebook. Also in the room were a desk and a chair.
There were several religious pictures on the walls. The single
stained-glass window depicted The Annunciation. The choirmaster
was preoccupied and didn't see Miguel at the door.

"Excuse me, Señor," said Miguel.

The choirmaster looked up over rounded spectacles. "Yes?"

"My mother called earlier about my being in the choir."

"Your name?"

"Calabrias."

"You have just moved here from Mazatlan?"

"From Manzanillo."

"Why do you want to sing in the choir?"

"I have always sung in a choir."

"You sang in Manzanillo?"

"At the Church of the Divine Inspiration."

The choirmaster shifted his spectacles and reached over to his desk for a sheet of music. "Let me hear you sing this scale," he said. He played a scale for Miguel and Miguel sang the notes. "Now sing this. Very good. You have a pleasant tenor. In the boys' choir there are fifteen others besides yourself. Their ages are from nine to sixteen. A few are here now; the rest go to schools in other districts and haven't arrived yet. You will report here each day no later than 3:30. Do you wish to begin today?"

"If I may, Señor."

"Very good. We have already begun to rehearse for the Celebration of Santa Teresa. Do you know anything about her?"

"Only a little."

"She is the patron saint of Rinconada, and the savior of our city. You have heard of General Pepe Malavista?"

"Yes, Señor. He was a bandit. During the time of Santa Anna he looted many of our cities. He was killed here in Rinconada."

"That's right," smiled the choirmaster. He sat back in his chair and closed his eyes slightly, then began speaking in a voice that was filled with both reverence and sadness. "The Gereral was leading his men into the city when a young flower girl of sixteen stepped in front of his horses. Though the hot road burned her feet, she offered the General a carnation from her bouquet. Malavista must have thought she was pretty, because he dismounted and took the flower from her hand. She asked him to spare the city in the name of the beauty of that flower. He refused and threw the flower in the dust, for his men were impatient; their horses were hot and thirsty. The metal of their gunbarrels burned their skin in the sun. 'All my life,' he said, 'beauty has been kept from me.' 'But why do you kill and rob?' she asked. 'I have always done so,' he answered. She begged; she asked him to spare the city for her sake. She said she would be his servant, but although the General wavered, he refused again. His men were spitting in the dust. He told her that she would be his servant whether he looted the city or not. But the girl had a pistol in her bouquet of flowers. She pointed it at the general and tried to pull the trigger, but it was a large pistol and she was too weak. One of Malavista's men shot her down with a single rifle bullet and she fell dead like a cloth doll.

"But the flower girl had stalled Malavista long enough. The townspeople had had time to assemble and surround Malavista's small army, carrying rifles and pitchforks. As soon as Teresa fell, a hundred shots rang out from behind the bushes and from inside the houses. They say that if Malavista had rallied his men, he might have defeated the townspeople. Instead, when he saw the young girl fall, with red blood on her white tunic, her flowers scattered in the dust, he just stood there and watched like a man gone numb. The woman who shot him said he looked tired and old. But when he was killed, the rest of his army scattered. That was over a hundred years ago.

"Teresa was made a saint, and this church was built for her. Its bell was fashioned from the melted-down canons of Malavista's army. The townspeople placed it high atop the church to be rung loudly in celebration of their freedom."

"I have heard another story, Señor. They say that once every twenty years, for repentance, General Malavista returns and rings the bell of Santa Teresa de las Carnaciones."

"It's not just a story, Calabrias. The last time it rang, I was a choirboy like you. That was almost twenty years ago, during the feast of Santa Teresa. It was the loudest, yet the most melodious sound I have ever heard. yet the top half of the bell tower was boarded up as it is today."

"But if the tower is boarded up, how does the Padre call the townspeople to Mass?"

"We have a new bell, set lower in the bell tower. For over twenty years, except for that one time, it has been the only bell to ring."

"Why is the old bell boarded up?"

"To prevent vandals from climbing the stairs and ringing the bell. It is too loud. It annoys the townspeople."

"Do you think that it was the General who rang the bell twenty years ago?"

"Perhaps it was."

"Do you think he will return again this year?"

"I don't know. The Padre says not."

"But it is tradition. It is in the heritage of this church and this city."

The choirmaster removed his spectacles and looked toward the ceiling. Finally he asked, "Do you believe in Jesus and the Virgin?"

"Of course."

"And is that not enough?"

"I don't know what you mean, Señor Ramos."

"Go out and meet the others. Tell them to stop that banging."

*   *   *   *   *

"Come with me," said Catalano. "I'll introduce you to the Padre."

Miguel had been in the choir for two weeks and was well liked, even by Catalano. Rather than trying for revenge, the cadaverous monitor respected Miguel for the trick he had played on him, much like one thief admires a good heist pulled by another thief. Miguel had seen the Padre only in brief glimpses. He was a small, red-faced man of about fifty or fifty-five who wore spectacles almost exactly like the choirmaster's. He moved quickly around the church grounds as if he were on wheels, his cassock brushing the floor. He stood when Catalano and Miguel entered his study. His puffed cheeks made him look severe.

"You are Calabrias," he said peremptorily. "I took the liberty of asking the choirmaster your name when I saw you lock the dog in the vestry. I removed it before it could soil anything."

"Padre, I . . ."

"I know that you've been mollycoddled into thinking that boys will be boys; that the pranks of the father may be passed on to the son. But here, Calabrias, you can forget these ideas. Here, there will be no more of these vandalistic goings on. You are here to sing in the choir, not to fool around."

"Yes, Señor."

"You must not play in the battlements or climb into the bell tower. When I say something to you, you must react instantly and obey unquestioningly.''

"Yes, Señor.''

"Have you understood what I've said?''

"I think so, Señor.''

"And you, Catalano?''

"Yes, Padre.''

"This is a house of God and must be treated as such. The Fiesta of Santa Teresa is a very important service, yet I have heard talk of bandits and murderers. The Fiesta must not be associated with hearsay and superstition.''

"But the General, Padre. It is said that he will come this year and ring the bell of Santa Teresa.''

"The General was an outlaw and a plunderer. The church abhors everything he did. These lies about the General will be stopped. The bell belongs to a bygone era and should be melted down.''

"But how can the stories about the General be lies, Padre? Many people say that they heard the bell twenty years ago. The older ones remember it even twenty years before that.''

"The soul of General Pepe Malavista is in Hell,'' said the Padre.

"Then who rang the bell, Padre?''

"Vandals; perhaps boys like yourselves who like to play pranks. But this year it will not happen. I personally will guard the bell tower. There will be no more worshipping false gods.''

*   *   *   *   *

Miguel and three others strolled in the shadow of the church. They sank down in the cool grass and rested their backs against the mimosa trees. Choir practice was over for the day and they were waiting for their mothers to pick them up. Miguel's mother worked late in an office. The other three boys had difficulties at home and were often left at the church for days at a time. Because of this, one of the cloister rooms was often pressed into service as a dormitory. Sometimes Miguel, too, would stay there. Most of the boys had at one time or another spent a night in the cloisters.

"Do you think the General will come?'' asked Felipe. He was

the tousleheaded boy of ten who had shown Miguel the way to the choirmaster's study on Miguel's first day. Felipe's mother liked to meet men and often left her son at the church while she went out looking. She made small but frequent contributions to the church for his care.

"That's only superstition," said Catalano.

"You mustn't say that," said the other boy, Rodriguez. "It may bring bad luck."

"Bah. The padre himself told us that there can be no ghosts that ring bells."

Miguel spoke to the two younger boys. "It is true that the Padre thinks that the General is a bad spirit. He said that he will guard the tower on the feast day."

"But he cannot guard against a ghost," said Rodriguez.

"No," said Felipe. "The General will come and ring the bell as he has always done."

The next day, Miguel took Catalano aside and told him, "I don't think the General will come."

"Why are you telling me?" asked Catalano. "You know that I don't believe in ghosts either."

"Because he must come. The town expects it. If not, kids like Felipe and Rodriguez will be disappointed. It is like fireworks to them and they don't have much else to look forward to."

"I still don't know why you're telling me things I already know."

"We must see to it that Malavista comes," said Miguel.

"You want us to be the General?"

"Tradition says that we must."

"And it would be a good prank."

They were standing in front of the church near the iron gates. It was twilight. A car approached and both boys looked over to see if it were his mother. The car passed, and Catalano picked up a stalk of grass and bit it.

"But think, Calabrias. They say the General did come twenty years ago. What if he comes again and finds us in the bell tower?"

"I thought you didn't believe in ghosts."

"We must be prepared."

"I don't think he did come twenty years ago, or any other year."

"But who rang the bell? Even my mother heard it all the way across town."

Miguel looked down the dark street for cars but there were none. Beyond, weeds and vines seemed to creep across the latticed window of a house long empty. "When I first came here, and even before, when I lived in Manzanillo, I believed the stories of the General. . . ."

"And now you don't?" asked Catalano.

"No," Miguel was standing near one of the trees, picking off bark.

"But who rang it?"

Miguel turned slowly and faced Catalano. "I think the choirmaster rang it. He was a boy our age twenty years ago and he has always lived in Rinconada. He was sad when I mentioned the General to him when I first came. He knew that the Padre will be on guard next week to stop anyone from entering the bell tower."

"We will trick the Padre somehow, and get into the bell tower," said Catalano.

* * * * *

The night was clear as the two boys slipped out of the cloisters and crept along between the bushes and the wall. Less than two hours earlier, the church had still been filled with the sounds of the feast—the laughing, the talking, the merrymaking—which had gone on far into the evening. It had been their reward for praying to Santa Teresa for another year. The service, too, was well attended, and the singing had gone well. The voices of the choir had blended perfectly and the people had joined in of their own accord, many of the songs having been passed down from generation to generation. Even the Padre, usually so austere, had laughed and joked as the food was laid out on tables set up on the lawn. Miguel had not known that there were so many people in the town. They had drifted away from the Old Section; moved their houses closer to the shopping centers and to the better, more modern schools. But for the Feast of Santa Teresa they had returned. The lower bell had rung again and again, sending its chimes drifting through the mimosa trees and the celebrating people like a fresh breeze. Now the only sounds were the night insects and the faint rustlings of the bushes and stalks of grass as the two boys moved carefully along the wall.

The bell tower had two levels that were connected by a plain wooden stairway. The entrance to the tower was always unlocked, and the boys had often climbed into the lower level and held secret meetings. The Padre had even showed Catalano and some of the older boys how to ring the bell to call the people to Mass. A doorway boarded up with thick planks—dusty with cobwebs and mold—divided the room from the other stairway leading farther up. The boards had been well secured with large nails but, earlier in the week, Miguel had managed to loosen enough of them with a claw hammer to give him room to pass through. He had even ventured upward and gazed at the bell of Santa Teresa. He had touched the rope, black with soot and dried bat dung. He had then replaced the heavy nails with lighter, shorter ones so that the boards were in the same position as before, but only tacked on.

"Calabrias."

"Shhh."

"Calabrias."

"What? And whisper lower. The Padre will hear."

"There will be no bell."

"What did you say?"

"The bell of Santa Teresa will be gone. The Padre will have taken it and sold it. That's why he doesn't want us in the tower."

"No, the bell will be there. Do you know what you have to do?"

"Yes."

"Go, then."

Catalano nodded at Miguel and stepped from the bushes. His dark blue choir robes made him almost invisible in the darkness. He put his hands in his pockets and sauntered past the entrance to the tower. He took several steps and was not stopped. He took five more; ten. Miguel, watching from the bushes very near the entrance, thought that the Padre was probably up on the first level looking east through the tower window. In that case he would not have seen Catalano, who was walking on the south side, in front of the entrance. Nor could he see Miguel, who was too close to the wall below. Wooden bars prevented the Padre from putting his head through the window and looking straight down. Miguel was jittery. He knew that he would be caught but he wanted to get to the bell of Santa Teresa first.

Miguel had been trying to estimate Catalano's steps in the darkness. When he had counted twenty-five, he heard a high-pitched scream and Catalano's voice crying, "My leg—oh Jesus, it's broken!" Catalano had done his part of the job. Miguel crouched lower. He heard from within the tower the sound of hurried boots descending wooden stairs. He looked around the corner just as the Padre dashed out of the entrance and ran toward Catalano.

"What are you doing out here, boy? Why have you breached curfew?" His voice was angry.

"I'm sorry, Padre," wailed Catalano. "I couldn't sleep and had to take a walk. I stepped in a sprinkler hole and I think I twisted my ankle."

Miguel, protected by Catalano's loudness, slipped into the tower. He was wearing no shoes, and was silent on the wooden steps. When he reached the first landing, he looked down but saw no one. He hoped that Catalano could keep talking. Perhaps he could even get the Padre to help him back to the cloisters. If this happened, Miguel could escape and the Padre could not expel him from the choir. He began pulling at the loose boards. He had taken out four and was preparing to squeeze through when a hand clasped the collar of his robe and jerked him back. Miguel was so frightened that he convulsed into shivers. He struggled to get away but an arm grasped him around the waist so that he could not move.

"Leave now, Calabrias, and I'll say nothing."

"Choirmaster!" Miguel looked around and stared in amazement.

"Leave quickly. I saw the trick you two played on the Padre, and he will be furious."

"What are you doing here, Señor Choirmaster?" asked Miguel.

"Guarding for the Padre, what do you think?"

"But you must let me into the upper tower."

"No, you must leave. If you are caught ringing the bell you will be dismissed from the choir, and I will get in trouble also."

"But it is nearly midnight. I must ring the bell before the new day. The General . . ."

"Get out!" spat the choirmaster in a fierce whisper. He pushed Miguel so hard that he nearly fell down the stairs. When he had righted himself, Miguel looked back up and saw the choirmaster fooling with the planks. Defeated, Miguel hung his head and walked down the last two steps. As he stepped outside he collided with the Padre.

"Another one!" cried the Padre. "And in your choir robes, too!" He grabbed Miguel by the arm. "What are you doing here, vandal?"

"Nothing, Padre. I'm not a vandal."

"Are you a lookout?"

"No, Padre."

"Who else is up there?"

"No one, Padre." But the cleric rushed up the stairs and Miguel heard muffled whispering. He waited by the bushes for several minutes until the choirmaster came out of the tower. Miguel went up to him.

"It was you, wasn't it?" he said.

"What do you mean?"

"You rang the bell twenty years ago."

"No."

"When I saw you just now in the tower you were in a hurry. I thought you were putting back the planks I took out, but you were really trying to take out others so you could get through."

"That's only a guess."

"Where are your shoes?" asked Miguel.

"I forgot them."

Miguel was saddened—not because the choirmaster was lying to him, but because his failure in the bell tower had prevented him from perpetuating the tradition to others, twenty years hence. They were walking toward the cloisters when Miguel stopped and touched the choirmaster's arm.

"It's not too late. We can still trick the Padre somehow. So many people will be disappointed. All of the kids are waiting on their cots in the sleeping room; waiting to hear the General give penance for the evil he did a hundred years ago. Let's . . ."

As Miguel talked, a resounding clangor suddenly exploded from the tower, covering them with sound. They stood paralyzed, looking up toward the high tower as the bell of Santa Teresa rang again and again, becoming more harmonic and melodious with each chime. It covered the church grounds in resonant peals; the vibrations spread out over the city like ripples in a pool. In the Old Section, lights flicked on in the few houses that were still inhabited, and people ran out onto their lawns in their nightclothes. The bell had put Miguel into a trance. His thoughts had left him like dreams in the morning. Throughout the city, people woke up and smiled and held each other. Those who had not been sleeping looked at each other in relief and nodded. Still the bell rang out as if the bell rope were being pulled by a maniac. When it stopped, Miguel looked at the choirmaster in amazement. They ran back to the bell tower. At the entrance they saw the Padre, staggering. His robe was covered with a flaky dark film, and his hands were pressed to his face. When he took them away, he left black trails on his cheeks and forehead.

Miguel whispered to the choirmaster and to Catalano, who had materialized beside them. "It was the Padre all the time, and the noise of the bell has knocked him silly."

Catalano stepped up to the Padre, who was still dazed. "Did you see him, Padre? Did you see the General?"

"Hmmm?" The Padre seemed to be trying to shake off his befuddlement.

"Who did it, Padre? Who rang the bell?"

"Vandals," said the Padre.

Silk and Other Fine Things

The young man was slumped in a chair in a darkened corner of the hotel lobby. It was long past midnight. He had just crushed out his last cigarette and was staring at the thin and winding stairway with a mixture of longing and trepidation. He was several days unshaven, but his clothes—a pair of dress cords and a rugby shirt—were only slightly wrinkled. He was drowsy, and as he watched the staircase it seemed to become thinner; almost snakelike. Its vermillion carpeting was brocaded with golden, entwined fleurs-de-lis. The young man supposed that these might be symbols, and that the symbols were probably bad luck. Twice now he had walked up that staircase and twice he had come down again. Quickly, emptily.

Suddenly, however, two figures appeared on the stairs. The young man came wide awake, but neither was the person he waited for. Only an old woman holding to the arm of a servant—a butler or chauffeur perhaps. The servant was blonde and heavily muscled. His face, tanned and hard like a dried riverbank, was expressionless. As for the woman, her face was as serene and composed as that of one who slept. They approached the young man without seeing him. Then the woman released the man's arm and spoke in a heavy Spanish accent.

"Bring the car around, Ellery. And be sure that it is warm enough inside before you come back for me." The chauffeur helped the woman into a chair near the young man, who moved his coat quickly out of the way.

"Excuse me," said the young man.

The chauffeur made sure his own coat was fully buttoned, then went out through the heavy glass doors.

The old woman's skin was darker than her chauffeur's. Her gray hair was put up in a bun, and the young man reflected that a palm reader might read volumes in the lines of her face. She was dressed in an old-fashioned manner, with a long and heavy green dress, high-laced shoes, and a spectacular silk lace shawl thrown over her shoulders. The shawl was embroidered with intricate representations of jungle life, both real and mythical. Through the folds of the material the young man glimpsed a black Christ nailed to a living tree. Serpents of all sizes twisted vinelike around bushes and boughs while a crocodile watched from a distance with gleaming red eyes. The woman's own eyes were pale in comparison, but moved quickly around the room, never seeming to come to rest. She inhaled deeply and closed her eyes. "May I have one of your cigarettes?" she asked. "Ellery will not let me indulge."

"I—I'm sorry," the young man stammered. "I just smoked my last one. I'll run out and get some more if you want."

The old woman sighed. "No, no. Ellery is right. But I'm interested in a young man who smokes cigarettes in hotel lobbies at two o'clock in the morning. In fact, I meet many interesting people in strange places and at odd hours. We have several minutes before Ellery comes back for me. Please tell me what you are doing here."

It wasn't unusual for the young man to agree to such requests; in fact his business in the hotel was prompted by a similarly odd circumstance. He felt somehow that his words would become part of the history inscribed on the woman's face.

"I had a girlfriend once," he began. "We were both law students and were compatible in other ways as well. We liked cats; we liked to eat in Japanese restaurants; we enjoyed racquetball, chess, banana daiquiris just slightly bitter, and soft music. That's how it started."

"The daiquiris and soft music?" the old woman smiled.

The young man eyed the woman cautiously. "Yes. One day her favorite singing group came to town. I didn't like the group much myself—I thought they placed too much emphasis on the visual—but after a few drinks I was ready to go anyway. My girlfriend had gotten front row seats and we chatted for a few minutes while we waited for the lights to go down. Then the group was introduced and sang several numbers. I don't know if it was the drinks or what, but I found myself becoming mesmerized by the group's lead singer, who swayed and moved her head as if in a dream. I looked at my girlfriend kind of guiltily, but she was transfixed too. The singer's voice, though not powerful, seemed to weave a spell that affected everyone in the auditorium individually. Her words were like soft love poems whispered in tender moments, and I was brought up in a home that appreciated things like that. And the woman herself was exquisite. Her face, her arms, and the soft V sloping down between her breasts stood out white as alabaster alongside her dark blue gown. Her hair was dark black and set in long, thin curls like the snakes on your shawl. Every man in the audience—and at least half the women—was in love with her, but she had eyes for me alone.

"I know what you're thinking," continued the young man quickly. "You're thinking that everyone must have thought exactly as I did. And you're right, but everyone else was wrong. It was me she was looking at, and when the last song ended I stood up and whistled for an encore louder than anyone. I saw my girlfriend looking at me strangely, but I didn't care. In that short hour, I, too, had fallen in love. When the encore began, something happened that shaped my life forever after. The singer bent down and sang the song to me. This time there was no mistaking it! She looked deeply into my eyes and I was almost overcome with her radiance. I could see the silvery flecks in her eyes, dancing like sequins, and I could count her perfect teeth. I knew my girlfriend was shocked because I felt her pinch my arm and draw away, but I paid no attention to her. All I wanted was to reach out and touch the perfect whiteness.

"Just before the song was over, she took the microphone away from her mouth and whispered something to me that I can't repeat but which meant that she wanted to know me better after the show. Then she stood up and took her bows. I felt my girlfriend pulling me toward the door but I shook her off like a leaf and pushed through the crowd as they filed from the auditorium.

"There was no dressing room so I waited near the door where I knew they had to exit. They pushed their way out quickly and in a large group so I wasn't able to get close, but I followed them to their hotel. I thought it would be hard to get her room number, but all I had to do was buddy up to the desk clerk and I was in like Flynn. But when I walked up to the room, there was a party going on and I was thrown out by someone's bodyguard before I could even get the singer's attention. I paced up and down the hall for hours but the door never opened again. Finally, I went back to my apartment and slept.

"In the morning, I packed a few things and drove to the next city on their tour. Again I sat in the front row, but this time by myself. And although the singer didn't whisper to me that night or on any of the following nights, neither did she whisper to anyone else."

The old woman spoke. "So you have been following her ever since?"

"Yes. It's been three weeks now, maybe more. I have almost no money left and my charge cards are at their limit. And I haven't managed to see her alone yet. Maybe tonight or the night after."

"And will it have been worth the cost?" the old woman asked.

"The sequins in her eyes were more than I'd ever hoped to see."

"We are very much alike, you and I," the old woman said. She drew her shawl closer to her and smoothed the wrinkles on her long dress. She looked over the young man's head, dreamily, as if remembering something pleasant. Then she spoke again.

"I was born in Panama, in a small town called Ocu. In the 1930s, when I was growing up, there were less than a thousand people living there, but almost all of us were artists. But instead of canvas and paint or pen and paper, we worked with needle and thread. We made lace, and very beautiful and intricate lace it was. This shawl I wear is an example. I became, because of the tininess of my hands, proficient in embroidering with silk thread. Many of the designs I worked on were handed down from generation to generation, but I also created many designs myself. And our work was in great demand—not only in the larger cities like Colon and Panama City in my own country, but in places as far away as Buenos Aires, Mexico City, and Palm Beach.

"All of our work was done by hand and in our homes, and all our homes were dark and dusky huts without electricity. We had to sit near the windows, where great streams of light would cut through the room like rays from the eyes of God. I want you to imagine us there in our houses of mud or adobe or sticks or combinations of all three—sitting on straightbacked wooden chairs and bent to our work. On a table before us were arranged all of our fine threads and sewing tools. In this manner we would work in silence, with only the tapping of the older ones' canes to distract us.

"You see, with the close, intricate detail our work required, and the dark, often candle-lit rooms, many of our townspeople became blind. It is ironic, is it not? Such beautiful work going on all around, yet many not able to see it. And here is something else: although we knew that we might become blind, we still worked at our craft. I myself became rich and moved away from Ocu."

A cold breeze blew across the young man's face and he looked around to see the chauffeur standing in the open doorway.

"Is that you, Ellery?" the woman asked. As she stood up and waited for her chauffeur to approach, the young man realized she could not see him. She, too, was blind, and he had not even noticed. Now he watched carefully and marveled at how this small woman had attuned herself so precisely to the sturdy body of her servant. With only his footsteps as clues, she reached out and found his arm at once. Looking in the young man's direction, she said, "We are too much alike for me to offer you advice. Even if I gave any, you probably would not listen. In this, too, we are alike." With this, she allowed herself to be led forward, walking stiffly and staring straight ahead.

The young man watched the woman's gown as it trailed along the carpet and disappeared out the door. He involuntarily reached for a cigarette but found none. He looked toward the stairway and gazed at it until he felt the color seeping from his eyes and flowing down onto the flowery, brocaded carpet. It was only when its designs seemed about to unravel into a single thread that he realized how tired he was.

Railroad Days

(for Bob Seger)

On the very hot evening of August 13, 1965, Jerry Farmer stepped onto a train without shaking my hand. Although he had boarded the same train dozens of times before, his mind was already clicking down the tracks.

"See ya," he said.

"Remember, now," I reminded him.

"Our rendezvous," he said. "Sure."

"Our reunion."

"Don't worry," he said. But it was like he was already gone— he stared at me but saw only the distance between us.

My house stands by itself now. Ten years ago, when Jerry boarded the train for the last time, it was part of a sprawling residential block of one- and two-story slatboard homes. They were slapdash affairs, thrown up mostly by unskilled dead army labor at the beginning of World War II to house officers. Hardly had the paint dried when the houses were abandoned. The dead officers and enlisted personnel were shipped overseas. In less than a month the booming military trade in Tallahassee dropped to nothing. But the army found a use for its newly constructed houses. Soon after the evacuation, the section was turned into a community of pregnant army wives. My mother was one of these; Jerry Farmer's was another. They were wives of men who were shipped overseas in the first mass bloodline to Europe, but lost somewhere in the transfusion. In one of the ironies of war, my father, Sgt. Thomas Collins, was on a troopship that capsized in a storm off the coast of Spain, spilling him into the horror of an infinite Mediterranean. Jerry's father, along with a hundred other Tallahassee-trained men, was on the same ship. They all drowned.

The bulldozers are at work across the street; I saw them when I came in: razing the foundations of those houses, the bulk of which have been carried away, board by termite-riddled board, by cigar-smoking men in flatbed trucks. Everything looks so desolate, so bleak. Yet the bulldozing is said to be an improvement. They are making room for new apartment houses for college students with rich parents. Jerry's house, on the southeast corner of the section, was one of the first to go. It was whitewashed slatboard like the rest, with one small bedroom and a kitchen. Jerry slept on a couch in the living room. When my mother ran off with the priest, I spent the night there. The couch seemed huge then.

I never wondered how my mother secured this house, the best of the lot. How did she rate two stories with a bedroom for each of us downstairs and two more upstairs we didn't even use? I can imagine what it was like when she moved in: bare walls, cold wooden floors, severe army furniture. What was a frightened eighteen-year-old girl to do alone in such a house? It makes me wonder for the first time about the circumstances that might have led to our good fortune. But it's pointless to think about it. My mother remarried long ago and left the state, a simple housewife at last. I remained here alone.

I write in the back upstairs bedroom, "the priest's room" we called it because of a theology student who lived here for years as a border. We also rented out the other bedroom, but never had as much luck with it, probably because it didn't have a separate door to the outside. Many other students lived here over the years but they no longer have names or faces for me.

I remember the priest very well. He was a huge man, six feet five or so and well over two hundred pounds. A soft talker and a studier. He would sit for hours in front of this window, facing the large tract of land behind the house that gave way on the right to railroad yards with huge monster-trains stretching back out of sight. Sometimes, when the trains had clacked slowly off, he looked out over the massive army barracks that had been converted into housing for students living on a shoestring. Alumni

Village, similar in purpose but of sturdier honeycomb design, now stands on that site, the barracks having been torn down many years ago. It is filled to capacity by students who can't afford the type of monstrosity that will soon be built across the street. To the many Indians, Pakistanis, Chinese, and artists of every color, the married students' village is the only refuge from absolute slum dwelling. Even this old house will soon be gone. This will be my last few hours here. Tonight I'm moving across town to a new house of red brick, a new neighborhood of shaded, Spanish-moss-garlanded minimansions with spacious lawns and antique furniture. It's sad, but it's something that I've been thinking about for a long time. The thinking, the planning, and the preparation have taken the edge off the sadness. When I was younger, the rumbling of the trains was like the flow of my own blood. Now their silence is deafening.

If I imagine that I'm the priest now, here at my window, I can also imagine seeing the two boys playing in the field below. It had been full of weeds before the army came, but farm equipment was soon commandeered to clear the area to make a baseball diamond. Near the edge of the house someone planted four poles strung with chicken wire for a backstop. The soldiers only had time to play once or twice, but of course the priest never saw them. Neither did I, for that matter; they were too quickly dead. Jerry and I recleared the field with push mowers and organized games of softball and baseball with the neighborhood kids. Sometimes, when we had no baseball, we'd swipe a tennis ball from the courts near the barracks and use that. But by that time most of the other families in the area had moved away. Only the Indians from the barracks were left, and the game was as alien to them as our clothes. We spent a lot of time hitting rocks with sticks, making a game out of it. Often we saw the priest watching us from the window.

The field was set up so that the right-field line ran parallel to, and only a stone's throw away from, the railroad tracks. But the tracks were separated from the field by a great gully that ran alongside the tracks and out of sight. We would sit on the edge of the gully and watch the trains as they loaded or as they shunted by; pitching stones across the ditch, letting fly and hearing the resounding thunk on the side of the boxcar. We could tell if the boxcar was loaded or not by the tone of the thunk. Those were our idle days, summer days while our mothers were at work. The last few preteen years.

"Sometime I'm going to ride on one of those monsters," I said one day, chewing on a piece of sawgrass.

Why don't we do it now?" Jerry asked.

"Hmmm?"

"Let's go sneak in and hide away until it moves."

"Naw." I had been talking bravely like the adventurer I have never been. Now I had been caught out. I had given Jerry an idea—the idea of his life as it turned out.

We had played in the trains before. On secret nights we had lounged on the sawdust beds in the dark boxcars, hopped in the engine rooms, scudded along the coal cars like dark wraiths; Jerry leading, probing, spurring me on to new heights of exhilaration. But we had never been on a moving train.

"Come on," he whispered, and scampered down into the gully. He climbed the hill to the tracks before he looked back and saw me lingering. He gave me a fierce look and I followed, slowly and with trepidation. Both of us knew that the train was about to leave, knew further that it would stop only once, to couple empty flatbed cars, halfway across town. Jerry had already opened a boxcar door by the time I pulled myself up the hill by grabbing handfuls of shrubs and grass runners. There was no trick to getting in a boxcar. We had, as I said, both done it many times before. But this time I was almost dead with fear. I got in the huge car for one reason only: not to disappoint Jerry. I didn't want to set a precedent, and following Jerry was the only tradition I knew. It was a hay car, already filled with its hard straw bales. I ducked behind the highest one while Jerry managed to close the heavy door almost all the way. Then he joined me just as, far away, we heard the couplings clatter. The front of the train started to move.

"Let's get out of here," I said.

Jerry looked at me with wide eyes. I see now that Jerry was

probably as scared as I was about our adventure, but at the time, I saw only determination, a blazing anticipation of a lifetime of such running, of cattle cars and Texas marshalls packing 45s. "I didn't close it all the way," he said. "That way we'll get some air and we can jump off whenever we want to."

"What if they check?" I asked frantically. "What if someone comes in here and finds us?"

"You know they never check."

I did know. We had spied on the track guards every day for eleven years. We minicked their lantern-swinging walks, we knew their yells. We even knew their names and the names of the engineers. They would sometimes, on sunny days when Duke Snider and Whitey Ford headlined the sports pages of the newspapers, leave their sidings for half an hour and toss the ball with us. Some could hit towering drives that traveled for what seemed like minutes and which came down with frightening speed. We emulated them, we compared them to our heroes in stance, swing, trajectory. Yet on the train these memories were forgotten. That they might find us was my topmost thought, and "they" were made up, not of the conductors and switchers we knew, but of nameless, stubblefaced gorillas with beefy, scarred hands.

When our boxcar began moving, my mind slipped into an uneasy oblivion of suspended worry. Jerry climbed to the door and watched the moving scenery. I lounged on the hay bales and thought about my father. Our fathers, Jerry's and mine, were the chronic subjects of our thoughts and speculations—not their faces or their fates, for we had pictures of them in round frames and War-Office notifications on stunned white paper—but their train journey.

It had been one of the switchers—I don't remember his name now—who had fixed that train ride inexorably in our minds one rainy afternoon. We had our sticks and were wandering along the gravelly trackbed. It had drizzled all day, but nothing to stay inside for. The trees beyond offered some shelter, but when suddenly, almost without warning, a torrent of freezing raindrops caught us in the open, a brake engineer's shack was the nearest refuge we saw. It had a foot or two of sloping eaves, and we could stay dry in the lee of the downpour. When we arrived, wet and panting, the railroad worker was already there, shaking off his checkered hat, then slapping it against his wet overalls.

"Who are you boys?" he asked. His voice was raspy, but he seemed pleasant enough. I had seen him before, but only from a distance.

"We live back there," I ventured.

"Sure, you guys play over by the barracks. You're the ones who throw rocks at the trains."

"We only *hit* the rocks," I lied. "With these sticks, see?" I showed him the ends of the sticks—cut off broomsticks—that looked like they had been chewed up by the vicious teeth of some large dog. "And we never play if the train is moving."

"A game, huh? How do you play?"

"We get a load of pebbles and just throw them up in the air and hit them from our first base line. In the ditch is a single, against the upper bank is a double, over the bank is a triple, and over the tracks is a home run. But we don't get many of those," I added hastily. "The rocks are little so they don't break our sticks."

"It ain't my train," the man shrugged. "Almost nobody rides the trains any more anyway. Trains are like dinosaurs," he said.

"Did a lot of people used to ride the trains?" Jerry asked.

"Sure, but it tapered off after the war. When the soldiers came home, what there was left of em, they just didn't want to go away again. Some of em said they'd traveled too much already. The others just took planes."

"Were you here when the war started?"

"Sure, I was here. These sidings were packed with soldiers. First they came to Tallahassee from all over, then they all pulled out again. Most of em never came back, but it was an exciting time. I know. I rode the trains in the first war—almost all the trains in Europe—but the most exciting train is the train that starts you off where you're going. Most of the soldiers around here were just kids, but they sat or stood as if nothing was gonna pull them off that train. And nothing did. The whole yard was full of soldier cars—too many for the depot. They stood around with their packs and their skinheads and their rifles, or they went to sleep in the gully there or in the boxcars, waiting for the whistle. The officers had seats up front; got to use the club cars and the sleeping compartments. I watched all the trains pull out, and I watched the looks of those young fellows just staring out at the scenery like it was the first or last scenery they'd ever seen. It didn't matter what it was—a tree or a sweetheart—they just wanted to be on their way. These trains are just shuttles for pulpwood now, or for gravel."

The rain let up and the brake engineer pulled on his cap over unruly white hair and waddled down the siding. His story remained. Years later, on that first illicit train ride, I smelled the hay, fresh but musty, as well as the lingering odors of previous cargoes: crates of apples, tires, burlap; and I wondered if the soldiers had smelled the same things a dozen years before.

The train hooted a warning and I jumped up from my hiding place. We were stopping. The train hadn't come to a full halt before I pulled open the door and jumped for a soft spot. Jerry called out behind me—I heard him as I was in the air—but when I landed I didn't stop. Although I skinned my knee on a buried rock, I scrambled up quickly into the bushes and looked out. Down the track I saw passengers looking out windows and railway workers scurrying about on the sidings. I saw Jerry jump out cautiously and break for the bushes. Someone shouted and we ran. Whether the man had spotted Jerry or was just shouting an order we never knew. It was enough for us to have heard it. For me, it was enough to keep me from boarding a moving train ever again. For Jerry, it was the beginning of a greater adventure.

"What did you jump off for?" Jerry asked, panting. "I wanted to go on to Monticello."

"You're nuts," I answered.

The memory of the raspy voice of the white-haired old man from the brake shack had flooded the boxcar and given me a chill of fear. A fear that someday I would be taken off somewhere and never brought back. I feared the exhilarated eyes he had described, the martyred eyes of fighters who could never return. For Jerry, the opposite happened. I saw it in his wild-eyed, single-minded determination as he stood near the boxcar door.

I'm through packing. Most of my stuff is junk that I'll have Goodwill take away. The furniture is old and worn. In this room dustballs are scattered across the floor like tumbleweed along with carcasses of dead insects—starved and trapped in the dusty debris. In a storeroom I found boxes of old mementos—photos, drawings I'd done in grade school, and an old loose-leaf notebook, the pages filled with my own child's scrawl. Records of our baseball games—Jerry's and mine—just outside the window here. I was the Brooklyn Dodgers, Jerry the Detroit Tigers. I remember the teams, both twenty-eight-man rosters, without having to look at the lineups. I *was* the Brooklyn Dodgers for many years. Carl Furillo, Sandy Amoros, Charlie Neal, Gil Hodges. I practiced switch hitting (so I could faithfully play Duke Snider and Junior Gilliam) until I was as good at one as the other. Here are their names, listed in nearly the same order each day, sometimes several times a day. There are also pages of numbers and statistics, which I was good at even then. The yellowing remnants of our rockball games. Sometimes, when Jerry wasn't around, I played by myself.

After our train ride, I seemed to play by myself more and more. I don't think I realized it then, but Jerry was growing up quickly. I was too, of course, but there was a difference. Jerry was *anxious* to grow up, to test his strength against something larger, more immovable than pebbles. In those last years he began talking about his father—a man he had never seen. He lost steadily at rockball, his mind more on the trains than on the game. He sneaked on the trains often after that, once riding as far as Atlanta before he was caught and sent home on a bus. But it didn't stop there. He studied timetables instead of box scores and found new ways of hiding on the trains. He'd say, "Listen, I'm going to Jacksonville today. Don't tell anybody. I'll be back on the nine-fifty tonight. You wanna come?"

"Naw."

"Will you wait for me out here before you go to bed?"

"Yeah, okay."

His mother worried, of course. She knew what he was doing,

but I don't think she ever let on to him. She was a kind woman, very frail—a woman who shouldn't have been left alone when the soldiers shipped out. Being several months pregnant in a strange town confused her. She always looked like someone who had been dropped at a stranger's doorstep and who had waited all her life to be reclaimed. My own mother, although about the same age, was harder, much more self-reliant. Patricia Farmer was a small-town girl who earned money by working in her mother's dress shop somewhere in Alabama when the war broke out, when formerly carefree men began to look for women who would miss them.

I remember Jerry's trip to Jacksonville vividly because it was also the night my mother ran off with the priest. When he boarded and hid behind boxes of appliances, I sat on the bank of the gully, watching the train as it moved slowly out. There were few passengers that night, so it was easy for me to recognize my mother, carefree and chatting, walking through a corridor to a compartment. The priest was with her; in fact he had a tentative arm around her waist, as if he were afraid she would slip away. I had only a brief glimpse of his face, but that was enough. It was as if he were staring deep into silent terror. Then they were gone.

I went into the house and made some eggs for my supper. My mother was still a young woman. I had seen her with dozens of men, but I was shocked at the idea of her with the priest. Where had they gone? I wondered, and when would they come back?

Jerry came back on the nine-fifty, and I slept at his house that night.

My mother and the priest were gone all weekend, and both changed during the trip. My mother was more thoughtful but more distracted as well, prone to snap at little things and then apologize. She kept going out on dates, but not with the priest. One night as I was doing homework I became aware of a noise eeking its way down through the ceiling. My mother was out, so the noise could only have been coming from the priest's room. I tiptoed upstairs and put my ear to his door. He was crying, sobbing into his hands or into a pillow. It was too eerie for me—a man in his twenties wailing like a little boy. I listened to him in awe until the noise became maddening, like a leaking faucet, and I had to run outside.

My heart didn't begin to calm down until I reached the gully. I sat there for what seemed like hours, trying not to remember the disconcerting noises from the upper bedroom. Instead, I thought about the troop trains, the standing dead soldiers, the vacant, yet all-seeing eyes. I saw the uniforms, the shining gun barrels; I even imagined the dead men laughing, snickering, elbowing each other, and telling dirty jokes. Soon, Jerry joined me on the bank, but he wasn't in a talkative mood and we stared out over the tracks for a while without speaking. It was I who broke the silence.

"I think the priest has the hots for Mama," I joked, but Jerry looked at me seriously, almost as if he were offended.

"Is she out again?" he asked.

"Sure. She goes out a lot." I shrugged my shoulders. Jerry looked thoughtful and soon got up. I followed him.

I didn't begrudge my mother her dates. Even when the men came home with her I rarely showed any disinclination toward them. I simply went outside and hit rocks. I don't think I was ever real to her. I was more a tangible memory that she had to feed with her own dreams and nourish and entertain like a fantasy. I didn't mind, but heredity can play strange jokes. My mother's genes have left me untouched. Instead, I have picked up from my father a grim sense of mortality and a terrible wish to avoid changes.

The next day I came home from school to find Jerry already sitting by the gully with the priest. This happened several days in succession. I was reticent to join them, but I often watched from my window. They seemed to have a lazy companionship: Jerry would toss rocks idly across the tracks or point out certain trains as they passed. But at times I saw something else—more serious discussions, silent speeches in which the priest would bang his hand down hard on the grassy bank. Jerry would ask a question and the burly priest would throw his hands up over his head as if he were plagued by hordes of tiny spirits. What were they talking about? I wondered. What could they have in common? The day I decided to join them, I came home from school to find that the priest had moved out.

Jerry's mother never remarried. She never even dated, although, after the war, many men asked her out. She preferred to do for herself. She had her job (as an alterationist) in town and she had her clapboard shack. And she had Jerry. Sometimes she had me as well. I would secretly study her at the dinner table or as we all watched Soupy Sales on Saturday morning. She never caught me because her eyes were always on her son, following nervously as Jerry lifted his fork, opened his mouth to laugh, or pointed to some object he wanted me to see. She looked at him as if she were seeing someone else in his eyes, and of course she was. I often compared his face with the face framed on the mantle, and she was right. I know what she was afraid of. I felt the same way.

We grew up, Jerry and I. We grew into young men and I watched Jerry board the train again, this time in his own army uniform. I watched his mother, almost forty then, crying for him without knowing it, treating her tears like troublesome locks of hair. I shook his hand stiffly, formally. So did the conductor and the old brake engineer that we had come to know so well.

"Come on along," he shouted at me.

I shook my head, a bit embarrassed, a bit disappointed that I was letting him down again. But I had gotten accepted to the university and I had new things to think about. We saluted each other awkwardly, and I walked out of the station.

Jerry came back. He wasn't a war hero but neither was he dead. His hitch was over, and I met him at the station. I remember thinking about how much like old times it was—him going off and returning on the train. And he looked good. Fuller, tougher, his face darker. But I was alone at the station. His mother had died in his first year away. He was stationed overseas and, through some administrative snafu, didn't get word of her death for nearly a month. It was the first thing he thought of when he stepped off the train.

"Thanks for taking care of Mama like you did," he said after we had greeted each other. "You know, there was nobody else here."

"Sure," I said.

"The priest," he remembered suddenly. "Did he say anything at the funeral?"

"The priest has been gone from Tallahassee for ten years," I reminded him. He was chagrined at his mistake and waved his hands helplessly. At the time, I thought it curious that he should think of the priest at all. But no longer. Jerry was looking back to a time before the priest had gone, to our railroad days and our rockball games.

We were thirteen when the priest finally gave up his room. He left suddenly, without saying goodbye to anyone. When I came home that day I asked my mother about it; where he'd gone.

"I don't know," she said, but she seemed to be caught in a rare befuddlement. Her eyes were rimmed with red and she didn't look like the fierce, carefree woman she tried to appear. For years afterward, I assumed that she was indifferent to the priest's departure, and that her tears were over another suitor altogether. Now I no longer opt for one or the other. The possibilities of the scene disconcert me. I was a nonchalant child, regrettably obtuse. Today, although I can picture the priest's lumberjack bulk, a leviathan in a mousehouse with a soothing, sometimes pouting voice, I do not remember his name. I'm not even sure I ever did. Perhaps he made a fine priest in time; that is, if he ever decided to enter the priesthood. Perhaps he became a soldier, I don't know. I assume he left Tallahassee on the train, although it appears now that I know nothing for certain.

I try to remember our games after the priest left, but I can't. Evidently Jerry and I wandered apart then, I to a more organized style of sport—Little League, Pony League—while Jerry drifted more heavily into his trains and his solitude. Nineteen fifty eight is the last year recorded in my score book: the year Brooklyn moved to Los Angeles. A dynasty was over. Duke Snider was a relatively old man; Pee Wee Reese had retired; Newcomb and Maglie had disappeared. The magic was gone from the game. It's only natural then, when I think of Jerry, to think of our railroad days together. I'm sure that if he thought of me, he thought of the same period.

Jerry returned from the army at a bad time for me—finals time—and I wasn't a good enough student to neglect any part of my preparations. I promised Jerry we would get together in a week or so. By then, I said, I'd have my degree and be able to take a rest. Jerry rented a room across town and I saw him only once. I was studying in the priest's room when a movement from outside distracted me for a moment. I looked out the window and saw Jerry standing on the bank of the gully, arms crossed and staring out at a moving passenger train. When I finished my chapter I went out to join him, but he was gone.

I was offered a job as an accountant by a Tallahassee firm as soon as I graduated. In the excitement of entering a new phase of my life, I forgot all about Jerry until, in the second week of my job, he arrived at my house. When I opened the door, I noticed a bulging duffel bag at his feet. His appearance struck me: his hair was cropped short and, with his square jaw, his face had a powerful contour. He had become a man in the army while I still felt like a shaveling.

"Come and see me off," he said.

"Where are you going?"

"To catch a train."

"Where to?"

"I'm going to leave it up to luck," he said. "I've got a ticket to Mobile. In Mobile I'll make another decision until I get somewhere that looks interesting."

"Come in and sit down awhile," I said.

"No, really; I have to be off."

I followed him into the driveway. "We can take my car," I said.

It was a hot, unpleasant evening. The humidity was stifling, and sweat ran in streams down our bare arms. On such a night I was glad to be spared the annoyance of having to walk.

"I didn't know you had a car," Jerry told me as he got in.

"I bought it at an auction," I said.

"It seems to run well enough," he said.

"Yes," I agreed, and was about to say more when I threw a glance at Jerry from the corner of my eye. His face had gone blank as he stared out at the built-up roads, the apartment houses, and the new residential neighborhoods that had sprung up in the years he was away. Suddenly I felt a horrible sense of guilt. My best friend, perhaps the only real friend I ever had, was leaving and it was my fault. I had been too busy to see him. He was restless and I had been unavailable. "Why are you leaving?" I asked finally, as we neared the station. "Stick around. We can have some good times. . . ."

"I know we could," he agreed. "Let's have a drink now for old times sake."

"All right."

We walked together into the terminal bar, Jerry with his duffel, I with my hands in my pants pockets. The bar, years past its heyday, had been reduced to a dingy little cubbyhole with four or five tables and a cigarette machine. A very dark and cheerless place. We both ordered beer and sat down at a table with our glasses.

"Here's to you and your new life," Jerry offered.

"To both of us," I corrected him. "You haven't told me why you're leaving."

"I'm just antsy," he answered. "Restless like a little boy. I walked over to the field the other day and watched the trains. It's like nothing had ever changed. I could smell the sawdust of the boxcars and it didn't matter that I was twenty-one years old or that I didn't have a job. I just knew I wanted to be on that train again. There isn't anything for me here any more. Maybe there never was. I want to say that I would have stayed for Mama, but I guess even that's not true. Mama was a stranger here too, and I think that's what killed her, the strangeness. The fact that her Alabama ways weren't any good in a university town. Your mother was smarter, maybe. She adapted, she survived. You're like her and you'll do well. I'm like a mulatto. I feel the strangeness of my mother and the wanderlust of my father."

A train—Jerry's train—hooted, and the platform announcer made a first call. "What will you do?" I asked.

"I don't know." He looked up from his glass and spoke seriously. "Remember the priest?"

"Sure," I said, remembering the huge man as he had looked
on the train with my mother: wide-eyed and scared. It was a disquieting memory.

I glanced up to find Jerry studying my expression. "People
are torn between things," he began hesitantly. Then he started
over. "I don't think that many people ever know for sure what
they want to do. That's why I admire you. You've never had
any doubts. I have. That's why I need to travel around—even
if I don't know where I want to go. I wanted to be a soldier once,
so I signed up. Just to try it."

"You could have been killed," I said, feeling shocked, but
curious.

"Maybe I wanted to try that, too," he said. "I used to talk
to the priest right before he left."

"I remember that," I said.

"I asked him what it was like to be a religious man."

"What did he say?"

"He said he didn't know."

"Well, I guess he wasn't a real priest. . . ."

"That's not what he meant. It was just the way he was. He
didn't have any other way to compare it to. I thought about that
for a long time. I thought about my father being killed before
he even reached the war. Nobody gave him any answers either."

"Why did the priest go off that night with my mother?"

"That's just it," Jerry said sadly. "He didn't know that either.
Listen, I'm rambling and the train's getting ready to go. I just
wanted to try and explain why I'm leaving and I can't."

"Maybe you'll know when you get where you're going."

Jerry smiled and put his hand on my shoulder. "I hope so,"
he said.

I hoped so too. In fact I suddenly hoped it desperately, but
I had no time to explore that hope as the last call resounded from
the platform. We finished our beers and walked out of the bar.
Jerry took his ticket out of his shirt pocket and moved toward
a coach.

"Can I look for you?" I asked.

Jerry smiled. "Trains go both ways," he said.

"Ten years," I suddenly called out.

"What?"

"We'll have a reunion in ten years."

"I'm up for that," he said.

"You sure?"

"I'm sure."

"Write down the date," I said, smiling.

"I've got it."

"We can have a little game," I said. "They've got a thing called a whiffle ball."

"That'd be great," he said. The announcer blew a whistle and Jerry stepped up onto the train.

"I'll be looking for you," I said.

"See you," he said.

The door closed and the train pulled away, slowly at first, then gathering speed, the bulky wheels making a thick metallic ringing on the rails as it passed. I hadn't taken his hand; a handshake would have signified too final a departure.

Darkness is falling quickly now over the railroad cars—those last few rusting hulks which have long since been discarded by the lines. Kudzu vines have encroached upon the field and now totally engulf the gully and the hill rising toward the tracks. Last year the railways had to douse the track beds with herbicide to stop the vines from growing around the tracks. Now the vines can do what they will. Telephone guy wires are covered by the vines, as are two or three old piles of gravel, dumped from a railroad car years ago. In the darkness, the vines look like formless monsters, the gully like a jungle in miniature.

They shut the trains down. No more passenger service to Tallahassee. There was no profit in it anymore. The warehouses have moved elsewhere along with the freight cars, and the tracks here will soon be deserted. Already the engineers and the maintenance people have been transferred. They will go where the trains go. Even I have a new home, although I will move into it alone.

Jerry didn't make our rendezvous. I wonder if he has settled down somewhere, gotten a job, a family. All I know for sure is that, without the trains, he will never come home. Sometimes I feel the ghost of my own father in me. I feel him now, in fact, curbing my restlessness, and I wonder if in my father's eyes there might have been a touch more fear—unnoticed of course among those idling, spitting soldiers—than in the others; a shade more despair, more hopelessness.

I had the electricity cut off earlier today, and shadows are beginning to cast a pall over everything here. Outside, the noise of the bulldozers has stopped for another day. I suppose I could have been more stubborn with them, held up construction for another year or more, but I have waited too long already.

I've been waiting for Jerry for ten years, but Jerry didn't come and I'm trapped alone with myself. I'm stranded in the same place I've always been. My mother has gone. The priest is a bulky, sad memory, and Jerry has found the wonders his father only dreamed of. What are those wonders, though? That's what I wanted him to tell me.

The Dead Hunter

I spotted the wake of a pygmy rattler in the high grass and leapt free. The mountain man told me that even a small snake can kill if it gets you near the heart. So I wore a thick woolen shirt, boots, and two pair of socks and went walking through the rose brambles and the timber garden. The path was covered over—no one had walked this trail since the old hunter had died. His cabin stood brown and still in a small clearing. Wispy clouds scudded above the chimney like smoke.

In a rock-filled stream I found the door to a Model-T Ford, rusted and muddied by the rain sluicing down from the mountain. Here and there were fruit trees, and I ate wild strawberries in an area so thick with vines that my hands were bloodied by the juice as well as by the thorns. I sucked my fingers dry.

Over the rise, my new cabin could not be seen, and if any cars passed on the road—somewhere up and behind me—I could not hear them.

I took some strawberries to the mountain man. "No game," I told him.

"You have to stay still," he answered, "and let the game find you. When your tongue hangs out like a leather belt in the sun, and your legs and arms feel like twigs ready to snap, the game will tell you stories."

"What about snakes?" I asked.

"Saw a king snake once," he said, "with a tail on both ends. I didn't know where to grab it. Then I saw that it was one snake eating another whole."

"It's a snake-eat-snake world," I said.

The mountain man cradled his rifle and brushed a hand through his beard. "No," he said. "The king snake was swallering a copperhead. It's the gentle snakes that survive."

I went out with my rifle the next day and the next, but still

I saw no game. Even when the rain washed the valley clean and caused the streams to flow more heavily, the hills and the trees seemed lifeless. I looked for the rusted car door, but it had been carried away by the rushing stream into some other time and place.

I pushed on through the brush to the old hunter's abandoned cabin and stumbled into a pit—a root cellar long unused. I fell on decades of cushiony leaves. The walls were stacked rocks, pushed shapeless by wandering earth. I looked down and saw the dark mulch of the dead hunter. I looked up and saw the mountain man. He looked down at me with a sharp eye. "There's your snake," he told me. The sun was streaming down into the pit like hot needles and I watched a diamond leaf move slowly off a rock wall, trailing its copper train. There was a report, like thunder, and the leaf turned red. The tail twitched, but the snake was dead.

"*I* could have shot it," I said, but the mountain man just shrugged.

"You're a young man," he said. "You've made that new cabin of yours snake-proof, but I saw the old hunter grab a rattlesnake by the tail and snap it like a bullwhip. Killed it dead."

"It's kill or be killed," I said.

"He lived for a week on that rattlesnake meat, and the skin was so big he could slip his whole rifle inside. He was seventy-two years old then."

"Tell me about other game," I said.

The mountain man reached in the pocket of his overalls and took out a snuffbox. "I knew an old boy once," he said. "I think he was from up around Fort Smith somewhere. We were both lying in a hole not quite a big as that one you're in now. This was in the Ardennes, back in the war." He took a pinch of snuff and put the box back in his pocket. "This old boy was nuts for hunting. All we'd had to eat for three days was some powdered eggs and a can of Spam. We was lying there, the forest and who knows what else all around us, when this feller says 'Squirrel!' I could see his mouth start to waterin and he took up his gun.

" 'Cain't be no squirrel,' I told him, but he said it was.

" 'I can hear it squak,' he said. 'It's probably up in one of those hollow trees.' He made sure his rifle was loaded. 'You got to be careful shootin squirrel,' he said. 'Otherwise when you kill one, it'll fall right back down in the hollow tree.'

"I suppose he meant to make a small fire and cook the danged thing after he shot it, but when he stuck his head up out of the foxhole, a German shot it half off. Old boy fell right back down in the hole."

The mountain man walked away with steps so slow and light that I saw a leaf flutter to his hat and stay. I was still chest-deep in the root cellar. I had not taken my rifle from my shoulder, yet I felt as if I had fired a shot at something dangerous and missed.

The Principle of Interchange

Waking up in this room is like waking up in moldy coffee. My skin is slippery with sweat, but my mouth is oatmeal-dry. It is early—the morning is still gray. My wounded arm is puffy and red. The sheets are on the floor again. They are stained with drops of my blood, as if trying to soak away some of my little horrors.

Last night was vicious.

There is a bloodstain on the doorpost. It was originally made by Dawn Wells, the previous tenant, but this morning the stain is larger, brighter, and uglier than it was yesterday. When I think of Dawn Wells, with her black hair whipping about in anger and frustration, her arms red and torn, I feel the helpless sadness of a meticulous man who hears chaos approaching.

I never met Dawn Wells, although I wish I had. Still, I have met people like her throughout my life and am beginning to realize that perhaps everyone would be Dawn Wells if given the chance.

I am—was—a policeman, a detective. I have seen people in the extreme stages of emotional exhaustion—drug addicts, assault victims, killers. I always thought that there was something the matter with their eyes and mouths; something strangely out of kilter.

Yet, emotion is new to me.

Laura once told me that being a policeman made me cold and bloodless, but she was wrong. I always regarded emotional outbursts and other evidence of inner conflict with suspicion, and this is what made me a good policeman.

Strange that I should think of Laura now, after weeks of singleminded, obsessive devotion to Dawn Wells. In fact, I have rarely thought of Laura since our divorce, over three years ago. The divorce seems significant now, as if it somehow began the pattern that eventually led me to this room.

I met Laura in Minneapolis in the winter, and we married quickly. I was a lab technician trained in paint and bloodstain analysis. She was a nurse. Judging from the state of my arm this morning, I learned nothing from her about first aid. It is to my discredit that I learned nothing from her at all.

We settled down happily, with a mild conviviality toward each other and a total dedication to our work—what work there was. We both brought home a fair salary, but while Laura had no end of accident victims to administer to, my work was dull and uninspiring. The time I spent analyzing the few materials I was given often went for nothing, due to incompetent inspectors and prosecutors. I longed to be in the field—to visit the crime scene—instead of sitting behind an electron microscope for a few hours a week and doing crossword puzzles the rest.

And my opportunity came. A woman was robbed and brutally battered. She had been grabbed by the hair and pulled into an alley. She was found half dead and rushed to the hospital. A suspect was in custody, but nothing of any value could be coaxed from his mouth or shaken from his clothes. He had a recent red puncture in his palm, but no other wounds or bruises. Where could a man get such a small wound? I reread the report but came up with nothing. I called Laura. It was the first time I had ever bothered her at work.

"Laura," I said. "Were you around when that assualt victim was brought in earlier today?"

"She's on my ward. Why?"

"Was she wearing earrings?"

"I don't know. Wait, yes I do. She wasn't. Isn't."

"Are you sure?" I asked.

"I had to get the blood off her face before we could treat her. She wasn't wearing earrings. Have you caught anyone yet?"

"Not yet. Well, maybe. I'm just trying to figure out . . ."

"Figure out what? And what are you asking these questions for? Isn't Sergeant Adams supposed to ask them?"

"Has he?" I asked.

"No; I don't know. Maybe he asked the doctor. You didn't answer my question."

"I'm tired of people botching up cases," I said vaguely.

"Still, they're the ones paid to do it."

"I'm a policeman too," I said.

"You're always saying that," she said.

"Look," I said. "Did the woman have any sewing in her purse, maybe a diabetic syringe, a knitting needle?"

"How would I know that?" she cried.

"Sorry, I'm thinking out loud. I'm looking for something that could have made a pinprick."

"A pinprick? What about a hatpin?"

"A hatpin?"

"The lady was wearing a hat," Laura said. "But it was as if it had been crushed in someone's fist, like somebody pulled her down by her hair."

"That's it!" I exclaimed. "Look. Don't move. Meet me in the lobby in ten minutes."

"Jim, you can't . . ." she began.

But I hung up.

I grabbed a few pieces of equipment and drove quickly to the hospital. This was action at last. Laura was waiting near the admissions desk. "Take me up there," I said.

"I tried to tell you! Her room is off limits to everyone except hospital personnel."

"I have to have a look at her."

"She may die!"

"Where's Adams?"

"He went to the cafeteria for a cup of coffee."

"Then I have to see her now."

"Why?"

"Look. When people commit a crime, they always leave something at the scene that wasn't there before, and always carry away something that wasn't on them when they arrived."

"What are you talking about?"

"That's the principle of interchange."

"Go to the scene of the crime, then."

"*She's* the scene of the crime."

"What?"

"I'm serious."

"You mean you might be able to convict someone . . ."

"Yes, of course."

"But why not just wait until the doctors give clearance . . ."

"It might be too late then."

"I don't believe you. You just want to solve a case on your own."

"No. Yes. What difference does it make?" I nearly shouted.

"You're putting me in a dangerous position."

"I have to do this."

So she took me up a staff elevator and let me into the woman's room. She was still unconscious, and her face was swollen and bruised, but that's not what I was concerned with. I first looked for patterned marks that may have been made on her cheeks by rings. I also looked for bits of skin under her fingernails, although I had no real hope of finding anything there. Laura was standing by the door, watching me. "Jim, hurry!" she whispered.

I lifted the woman's head and piled her graying hair on the pillow. Using my fingers I combed through the disheveled mass, studying each lock with a magnifying glass. I soon found what I was looking for—a small stain of blood, then another. I snipped off one of the stained locks and put it in an envelope. I glanced at her chart—Blood Type O.

"Jim . . ."

"I'm through," I said.

I managed to leave the building without any of the investigating officers seeing me, and drove back to the laboratory. My analysis of the blood showed Type B. A sample of blood was taken from the suspect and I found that it, too, was Type B.

"That don't mean beans," Sergeant Adams said. "Lots of guys have Type B blood."

"Do lots of guys also have an additional type MN, with the Rh negative factor?"

"What are you trying to say?" he asked.

"There's not just one blood group, there are six. The chance of him matching out on any three are pretty slim."

Because of my evidence, the suspect was convicted, and I was promoted into the actual workings of the police force. I divided my time between street investigation and lab work. Yet as my job satisfaction grew, my relationship with Laura deteriorated.

"You're a machine," she said one night about a year after my first promotion. We were eating a fast food dinner before having to rush back to our respective jobs.

"What are you saying?"

"How can you read an autopsy report over dinner?"

"You're a nurse. You're used to roughstuff."

"I try to leave it at the hospital."

"I like my work," I said.

"You're morbid."

"I'm just dedicated."

"Your own principle is destroying you," she said abruptly. I put down my report. "How so?" I asked.

"Murders, beatings, rapes: they're all horrible, brutal things committed by cold and unfeeling people. That's what a killer leaves at the site of a crime—a coldness, a disregard for life. Every time you investigate something, some of that coldness sticks to you and you can't shake it off."

"It's more complicated than that," I said. And it is.

She left me and married a more compassionate man. After the divorce I transferred here. A bigger town, with more responsibility and more people. More crime.

I open the curtains—frayed and ochre-colored—and look out into the street. Only a few cars make their way through the gray haze. Strange, but I don't remember ever looking out on this street before. The weeks I've been here have been weeks of closed curtains and wild introspection. I suddenly have a beard and my hair has grown unkempt. Clothes are strewn about the floor along with empty cans of beans—their jagged lids leaning toward me like faces.

My arm hurts. The skin throbs, but it seems to be someone else's pain, not mine. Yes, I can easily visualize it as Dawn Wells' pain, and that is comforting.

During the last weeks I have studied the bloodstain on the door-post. With my training, I can determine how long it has been there and how tall the person was who made it, but I knew all that before I even walked into the room. My imagination supplies the difficult part.

Before coming to this room I was chief investigator of the homicide division. I spent most of my off-hours in the laboratory, or reading up on new lab techniques. I was considering teaching a class on forensic science at the university and putting part of my fee toward updating some of our equipment. But something intervened between the planning and the action. His name was Smith.

Smith was a graying man in his fifties and a licensed private detective. As he walked into my office he nearly stumbled over the rug, and his hat fell off. "Excuse me," he said. "Am I bothering you?"

"Yes," I told him.

"Well, then," he said, stuttering slightly, "Well then I have something for you anyway." He stood in front of my desk, hat in hand. I scrutinized him carefully and quickly.

"You need to be in another profession," I told him. "A man your age should eat better, should have a new coat."

"I know that, Mr. Turner," he said. "But this profession is all I have. I've been bad at it for thirty years, but now I've done something lucky."

"What is it, then?"

"Did you know there is a prostitution ring here?" he said.

"In this city?" I asked.

"Yes, and it's widespread, too. It involves politicians."

I had heard rumors of "escort agencies" for state senators and representatives when the houses were in session, but I had never believed them. What purpose would any of these high-profile faces have in jeopardizing their careers?

"I don't believe it," I said.

"It's true," he said. "I have pictures."

"Pictures?"

"A videotape," he said. "I shot it last night."

"I want to see it."

Smith brought in his equipment. While he was setting up, he

told me how he had stumbled into the racket while acting for a woman in a routine family matter. In the course of the last few months Smith had isolated a member of the escort service, who he had learned was a student at the university. Her name was Dawn Wells. That's all he told me before he switched on the machine.

"I had to put myself in hock to rent this equipment," he told me. The picture, blurry and jagged, veered wildly before focusing on a pretty, darkhaired young woman of twenty-three or so.

"I've followed her home with guys, ten, twenty times," he told me.

"All women bring their boyfriends home sometimes," I said, preparing myself for a hoax of some kind.

"Not boyfriends like these," he said. The camera suddenly focused on a man taking off his coat, and just as suddenly my hoax theory went out the window. The man was a detective in my vice squad. I was visibly startled, but Smith didn't seem to notice.

"I waited for months," Smith said. "for the apartment next to hers to get vacant. When it did, I rented it. I broke into her room to check the layout. I peeled back the wallpaper and cut holes behind her mirror. I replaced her mirror glass with two-way glass. Then I waited. I know none of this will hold up in court, but I wanted to convince you . . ."

"Convince me of what?" I said. "That you're a good detective?"

"That it's not all just . . . Listen, there's something wrong somewhere. I don't know what it is, but it's getting worse. Everybody's going nuts. I believe in the law. It's kept me going for thirty years. But sometimes the wrong people go to jail because the law gets twisted. Or maybe it's been twisted all the time. Maybe I've just never seen it until now, but I wanted to show somebody else. I thought maybe that you . . . I don't know. I was lucky."

Yes, he was lucky.

The screen showed a relatively small room with a sofa-bed and flowery wallpaper. A kitchen was set into the back of the room and a door to the right signaled a bathroom. A voice came over the tape, indistinct at first.

"Look, maybe this isn't such a good idea." The voice belonged to the most striking woman I have ever seen. She was nearly six feet tall, with shimmering black hair that reached her waist. Her eyes were as hard as two almonds and her thick mouth produced a voice that was deeper and rougher than I would have guessed.

"What do you mean?"

"I usually don't do this with cops. It's a habit."

"This is a special case."

"They're all special cases."

As the man took off his clothes he began to look less and less familiar to me. He was tubby and very white, with acne on his back. Dawn Wells was shapely, dark-skinned, and beautiful. I was drawn to her face again. As her opposite buried his head in her neck and concentrated on his pleasure, Dawn Wells was free to show the hate and loathing she felt. Throughout his performance, her eyes remained open, staring fixedly at a point on the ceiling. When he finished, her expression didn't change, and he shrank back away from her. He put his clothes on quickly. This seemed to give him back some of his composure.

"I just do what society demands," he said.

"Society demands that you use people like they were toys?"

"I'm not the one that's for hire," he said.

"Aren't you?"

"I'm a good policeman."

"Sure."

"I'm a good policeman, but I don't believe in victimless crimes."

"It's not a victimless crime, and I'm not the one committing it," Dawn Wells said.

"How long have I known you now? Four months? Five?"

"I guess so."

"And have I ever busted you?"

"No."

"And how many times have I told you to get out of the business?"

"Maybe you should have been a psychologist, then."

"I mean it. Someone's going to get you sooner or later. Then what? You want to go to law school, for god's sake. Do you know what a conviction will do for your chances of getting admitted to the bar?"

"It's all I know how to do."

"Learn something else."

"What do you think I'm trying to do? But I'm twenty-three years old and just starting college. No one will hire me for a decent job because I've never had a decent job before. The only thing I've been good at is having people pounding my body."

"All people aren't bad," he said.

"Yes, they are. Do you think I want to work secretary jobs where I'd get goosed or patted on the ass as a reward for doing good work? Why shouldn't I become a prostitute?—I'd be treated like one anyway. Why shouldn't I get paid for it? Look at you with all the money in the world. Did you ever have a moment's doubt about being successful? A college education, a good job on the force? I was protected all my life, and taught to accept protection as all I had coming. Success? Success was having enough protection. Who needed an education for that? I was an Army brat. I had the whole U.S. Army for protection and I hated every second of it."

The man took a pack of Marlboros out of his coat pocket and lit one. Then he offered one to Dawn Wells, who shook her head. He tossed the pack on the bed and said, "Still, you got away from all that somehow."

For the first time, Dawn Wells' features took on an expression other than one of disdain. It was pensive; obviously his words had triggered something. Without replying, she got up from the bed, whipped her hair back out of her face, and slipped on a chiffon robe.

She lit a Marlboro from the pack on the bed and sat down at her dressing table, studying her face through cigarette smoke. Suddenly she turned back to face the man. "I got away all right. I got married. How's that for a first act of defiance? The only trouble was that my husband had been told about protection too.

Lucky me! I was soooo safe. But there wasn't anybody to protect me from him when he started beating me up. Not even the
U.S. Army would do that because he was my husband and he
had a right to beat me up. It was his payment for protecting me.
So I had to run away from him to look for some other type of
protection while he went off looking for somebody else to beat
up—I mean to protect. I was twenty-one years old and ready
to kill myself. And with every reason."

"I'm sorry," said the man.

"I don't need your sympathy," said Dawn Wells. "Maybe
I did then, but not now." She crushed out her partially smoked
cigarette in an ashtray on the dressing table. "After I left my
husband I got jobs in dime stores and cafeterias, then in bars.
I never made any friends because I always got fired too quickly
and do you know why? Because every time some asshole tried
to touch me I smacked him. I ended up in Nevada where I got
a job as an escort. It was legal there so at least there was no pretending that I was paid to do anything but fuck. After a while,
me and another escort went to Alaska and made big bucks giving blow jobs to roughnecks in bathrooms. Fifty dollars for five
minutes. I got to be a real pro at it. You know what *she* got?
A free plane ride to the north slope and a free gang rape. Then
they dropped her in the tundra so nobody would find her. But
somebody did find her and she's still alive, although she had to
have most of her fingers cut off because of frostbite. How's that
for payment? So I came here with my big bucks. At least I won't
get frostbite here. But big bucks go quick when you fly three thousand miles. I have to live in a pig sty and eat mold. What do
you want from me?"

"Nothing."

"Why did you come here?"

"Look, I'm an energetic man. I'm also an ugly man. I don't
get a lot of pleasure out of life. It could have been worse. Some
cops are shakedown artists. I've paid you the going rate. . . ."

"Until the next time."

"There won't be a next time. I'm a policeman first. Pretty
soon someone will find out about you—all of you, and all your

regular clients. I've even seen someone following you around."

"A client, maybe."

"Too shabby for your kind of client. Listen, I want you to know something."

"What's that?"

"I came here because of a fantasy. I've always wanted to make it with someone as beautiful as you. It was just something I had to do."

"Thanks for nothing."

"But it didn't make me feel as good as I thought it would. In fact, it makes me feel like shit."

"You want a refund? Forget it."

"I want to have the choice over again. But we don't get that, do we?"

Suddenly the picture wavered and jolted, and both Dawn Wells and her client jerked their heads toward the camera. Their faces went out of focus and flowers seemed to fly off the wallpaper and careen around the TV screen that Smith and I were watching. Everything was a blur of movement—the ceiling, a close-up of a lamp, the man running from the room in terror. Dawn Wells was screaming, but there was no longer any sound.

"What's happening!" I shouted.

The picture went blank. Beside me, Smith turned off the videotape machine. "I got spooked," he said. "A roach ran across my arm and I jerked the camera too far foward. I knocked the mirror off the wall and they could see the camera."

"So they know they were being photographed?" I asked.

"Yeah."

"Who else have you shown this to?" I asked.

"No one."

"Leave me the tape," I told him. "I'll get in touch with you later."

"Sure." He stood up to go out.

"Listen," I said. He turned around. "Most people who take pictures like this do it for blackmail."

"I know that," he said, and closed the door behind him.

I drove to Dawn Wells' apartment with only half a mind. It

wasn't my kind of investigation, but I was stuck with it. I knew I had to ask all the proper questions, to ferret out the elected officials who were making a travesty of the law. Without law, of course, we have nothing. I had little hope of success because I was certain that Dawn Wells had already fled the apartment and probably the city as well. As it turned out, I *was* too late, but that's because Dawn Wells was dead.

When no one answered my knock, I went into the room Smith had rented and looked for the hole in the wall. It had been covered from the other side with masking tape which I had no trouble removing. Evidently the mirror, or what was left of it, had been rehung as well, because I heard a thud as I tore away the tape. I was worried that the falling mirror might have startled her, but Dawn Wells had decided to accept no more surprises. She lay fully dressed on the rug; blood formed a red aura around the upper part of her body.

I stood still for several minutes. I was struck numb by the tragic unexpectedness of the situation. The flowers on the wallpaper—red roses, white dogwoods, purple peonies—went right on blooming, but Dawn Wells was dead, and from the first glance it was obvious that it was a suicide. Her wrists were cut cleanly and deeply. Small drops of blood were scattered around the room, as if she had gone to various places straightening up small untidinesses.

The door was unlocked. Even as I had been watching, on tape, Dawn Wells flinging out more emotion than I had felt in my lifetime, she had been lying here dead. Why? Because she had been discovered? Because all her hopes had shattered like the mirror? Because of a roach? It was unthinkable. There must be more. She had been discovered plying the only trade she knew, and suddenly I discovered myself doing the same. Like a thing apart, I saw myself standing in the doorway, my eyes moving mechanically over the room, noting each small detail—the made bed, the dishes on the rack in the kitchen, the pieces of mirror swept up and placed in a wastebasket by the door. Had she cut herself with one of those jagged pieces? It was too much. I was a policeman; it was the only thing I knew how to be. The most beautiful woman I had ever seen had cut her arms into ribbons and I was desperately looking for a culprit. I felt so disgusted with my own figure in the doorway—eyes clicking around the room like a camera—that I understood for the first time why some people might consider suicide. Some people—myself maybe—but not Dawn Wells.

They took out the rug, but I can still remember her exact position, a cloth doll thrown down right here where I now stand. The blood spots told another story: how she must have paced up and down the room before finally growing too weak to stand. At one point she rushed to the door and lay her bleeding wrist across the post, as if one part of her was begging the other to seek help. I have been studying that stain for the three weeks since that other part refused.

It is roughly roseate, with edges like petals where the blood must have welled up as she pressed down. It's as if one of the flowers from the wallpaper gained a brief moment of freedom.

I called in the crime lab, and they took everything away. The official report called it suicide, and I went home. Of course it was suicide. An idiot would know it was suicide. What I wanted the medical examiner to tell me was why. I went out and bought an expensive meal, but when it came I couldn't touch it. I kept thinking of Dawn Wells' bitterness. I thought of the horrible frustration she must have felt while waiting to die. And what was the cause? I went over it dozens of times and the cause was always the same: the law. It was way too much. The law was supposed to prevent senseless deaths, but it had caused the most senseless death of all. There had to be more to it. I lay awake all night thinking that there must be more.

In the morning I came back to the scene of the crime. The landlord was scrubbing the floors, getting the room ready to rent again. "I'm not through here yet," I told him.

"But you said . . ."

"Forget what I said."

"I have bills to pay."

"So do I."

It was I who found the note in her purse. It was folded up

in her wallet and heavily creased. I can see her taking it out whenever she felt depressed and looking at it, reading every word. It is a piece of notebook paper crammed with one sentence repeated over and over. The sentence is: "I will be happy." I have counted the repetitions. There are 206. Sometimes, one of the words will be underlined, but the underlined word changes. "I *will* be happy. *I* will be happy. I will be *happy*." It is like a schoolgirl's punishment at having done some minor wrong. Yet in this case, the punishment could not atone for the predicament.

I installed myself here. At first, I called in sick; then, as my moroseness grew, I arranged for a leave of absence. I am a forensic scientist, and my job is to find crime. And so I am. The note was my first clue, but the second was not long in following.

I had not been here long enough to begin biting my nails when Dawn Wells received a letter. I spotted it one day as I brought a batch of clean clothes over from my other apartment. The writing on the envelope was large and uneven, as if written by someone with a broken arm or wrist. I opened it and read it lying on the bed.

> Dear Dawn:
>
> How's my writing coming along, hey? not bad for a lady with flippers. I'm thinking about joining a sea-quarium. Actually, I'm using my prosthesis and I'm getting pretty good at it.
>
> We're a weird sort, you and I. I lost my fingers, but you're the one who's still helpless. You get pregnant, but I get the kid. It's a nice arrangement. Very nice. My disability is coming regularly now and sometimes I can sneak a few extra bucks by renting out the other bedroom. Janey's a nice little kid. Pretty, like you. She'll probably be talking soon, and I can't wait. The only problem is that she'll have to, someday, grow up. Write me, okay?
>
> Carla

I've read the letter so much that the words have started to look unfamiliar. I don't have a picture of Carla in my mind—that would be asking too much of a policeman—but I feel I know her voice as absolutely as I know Dawn Wells'. It's a bit deep, throaty, with just the trace of a laugh trailing behind each sentence.

I haven't written to Carla to tell her of Dawn Wells' death. I must do it soon, maybe tomorrow. There is also the legal problem of Dawn Wells' child, Janey. I assume that Carla is pretending to be the real mother.

But what will I tell her? "Dear Carla, Dawn Wells took her own life on Tuesday, May 16th, at 8 p.m. She had just been photographed in the act of committing a felony with a member of the vice squad. . . ."

That is what happened, and a month ago I might have composed just such a letter. Now it's impossible. Dawn Wells was not set up by the vice squad officer. He genuinely liked Dawn Wells. Perhaps he even loved her. He resigned from the police force without my asking. He can go to work in his father's business. I can't. I have chosen to live with it. Smith, wrong-headed and stumbling, also felt very strongly about Dawn Wells. He wanted me to help her, but instead he helped kill her. The one thing he ever did right was the investigation of Dawn Wells. Even now the papers are full of scandal about the prostitution ring. Senators are coming out of the woodwork like roaches to confess indiscretions. They don't concern me now. Nothing does, except maybe Janey, Dawn Wells' child. But if not for Janey, would Dawn have been driven to such despair?

Dawn, Smith, and the vice squad officer all inextricably entwined. Each desperate to do one good thing in their lives.

Questions still haunt me: Where will I go now? Back to my apartment? Back to work? To Alaska? I came here with preconceived and well-tested ideas about truth and about my purpose in life. Now I'm sure of only one thing: that I have been living my life wrong. I do not yet know how to live it right.

Last night I cut my wrist with the jagged edge of a can of beans, and watched the blood trickle down my arm and onto the floor. It is an ugly cut, but not deep. I watched until the blood began to coagulate, then I placed my arm over the doorpost so that my blood mingled with the stain already there.

Laura would have invoked the principle of interchange. The criminal brings something into the room of the crime—a cockiness perhaps, but perhaps something more tangible like a smear of blood. And when he (and I use this word with care) leaves, he takes away something that he didn't have when he came in: a wound, indecision, guilt.

But what is the crime?

Who is the criminal?

I ?

Killing the Assassin

I watch the assassin through half-closed curtains. It's a dark night and the landscaped azaleas, now in bloom, hide me well. The huge garden affords hundreds of such hiding places, but for my job I need only one.

The assassin has been paid to kill the man who lies sleeping before him. I have been paid to stop him.

The assassin knows no danger. He gently unbuttons the man's pajamas and carves "1 more" on his sleeping victim's belly. I admire this; this is good work. His knife is whisper-sharp and the man feels nothing. His muscles, like fat slugs, twitch under the huge belly.

The victim is a distasteful man and should be killed, but my personal feelings about him do not matter. Or, rather, they matter only to a point. I want to watch the assassin work. He is a black man and his features complement the darkness. Quick as a shadow, and as silent, he gags his victim awake. The victim's eyes are two coals of terror.

The assassin is a creative man. He ties a hangman's knot around the fainting victim's ankles and hoists him from a roof beam. He is a slaughterhouse butcher working the great meathooks, but he is also a sexton pulling a bell rope. He pulls until the victim's eyes are level with his own. The man's throat is puffy and round like a cantaloupe. The assassin's teeth and knife gleam, sending secret signals flashing.

Above me the moon breaks out from its cloudy prison. Around me the azaleas puff out their chests like *contras* before a firing squad, proud of their deeds. Like the assassin they are beautiful. Soon they will be dead. It's time for me to act. Although I wish the assassin no ill will, I crouch and take aim. As the assassin raises his knife, I cock my pistol, but in the same instant, behind me, I hear another hammer click back.

The victims, the assassins, all freeze. Behind us, the clicks echo forever.

Muffy

I was standing with my back to the bar watching someone I'd been in love with for six years dancing with drunks. She wanted no part of me—hadn't, in fact for most of the six years. I looked away and tried to concentrate on the band or on the other people on the dance floor, but her bobbing head kept surfacing like someone swept overboard in a storm. She looked ravished and satisfied. Her eyes were closed and her face was frozen in a rapture I couldn't believe in. I suppose that's why I was there, because I couldn't believe it, but enough was enough. I walked out and into another bar next door, the Foam Dome. In this bar there was no band; only scattered tables of scattered men and women. I stood by the cigarette machine with a beer. I felt sad and I wondered how long it would be before I got over it this time.

I was watching the door when Muffy walked in alone. It wasn't unusual to see Muffy alone; she's one of those people whose mouth has a mind of its own and revels in the prim putdown and the cold sarcasm. And Muffy, owner of said mouth, finds herself friendless. We were taking the same night class in poetry and knew each other slightly. Although I had a streetcorner interest in knowing her better, other things always seemed to intervene. For one thing, I'm too shy; for another, I was overwhelmed by her haughtiness and irony. Others, like the tall woman dancing obliviously next door, had taught me that I was nothing special. In fact, Muffy's whole appearance was cold—very pale skin surrounded by curly black hair, long, shiny, and perfectly groomed. Her thin face made her longish features very pronounced. Her mouth was small and angry. She looked like someone who, having asked for a night on the town, had been taken to a stag show. She always looked like that. Still, among the Evelyns and the Buddys in this Tallahassee bar, her mauve dress, muted just enough to appear casual, stood out like her name.

When she saw me she scowled, but came over anyway.

"I thought you went to New York," I said.

"For what?" she asked.

"To make your living as a poet."

"Oh, that," she replied, putting her fifty cents in the machine and pulling the Benson & Hedges lever. "I'm not ready yet."

"I thought you were the best," I said.

"Around here, Peter," she said, tearing a hole in the bottom of her package of cigarettes, "being the best doesn't mean much."

Muffy took a cigarette from the bottom of the pack and lit it. "What are you doing here?" she asked.

"Just bumming around."

"You look like shit," she told me. "What have you done to your hair?"

"Nothing."

"That's the problem. Do you play pool?"

"No, but I can watch a good game."

"Come play, then. I want to beat someone."

We got a table and a pitcher of beer and played. She won the first game of 9-ball easily. "You look like a real bum, you know that?" She spoke without looking at me; she was rolling her cue across the green felt to test it for straightness.

"So what?"

"Aping the bohemian writer?"

"I used to but now I'm too busy."

"Yeah, it looks like it. You break."

I broke, but not very well. She shot, missed her ball, but got in another. "It's the atmosphere," she said.

"Hmmm?" I shot for the 1, missed, and got the 3 instead.

"Nobody can seriously think of making it in Tallahassee. It's incredibly boring here."

"Why don't you leave, then?" I said.

"I told you. I'll leave when I'm ready."

I started a run of two or three balls, even though I was more than halfway drunk. While I shot I heard about how she had grown up on Riverside Drive in New York City, had known the poets A, B, and C, and had once lived with the best playwright under thirty on earth. I hardly listened. Or rather, I had heard it all before. After a while such references become like old addresses, and I had found that one place was as good as another.

"People are so unbelievably uncultured here," she said. She went on talking as she played, but when you're sick and dulled and you're about to look for an alley to sit down in, you find that you enjoy any conversation at all. Looked at in the best light, I was talking and playing pool with a cultured and attractive young prima donna. I was grateful for her company. I heard the dull bass of the band next door in the Rumpus Room, but it didn't bother me much at all. I looked at Muffy and smiled. When my turn came I made a great shot on the 8, but the cue followed it in like a sleazeball after a prostitute. I racked them up and watched her break. She squinted one eye and jerked her cue forward in a miscue.

"Relax your grip," I told her. "Let it slide easy."

"I know how to do it."

She beat me again.

*   *   *   *   *

I had written a poem about tennis, which the class had made noncommittal comments on. All except Muffy, who hadn't commented at all. After class, though, she caught up with me in the hall and started talking.

"You seem to know a lot about tennis," she said.

"Pretty much," I admitted.

"You were probably, like, great in high school, right?"

"I was okay. Do you play?"

"I had lessons when I was twelve just like anyone else on my block. It was okay, but I'm just not into athletics, you know?"

"Well, maybe you'd like to play sometime anyway?"

She looked at me suspiciously. "Like, when?"

"Anytime. Right now."

She hesitated. "No, I'd probably collapse. Why don't we go somewhere for a drink instead?"

Now, I hesitated. "I think I drank enough the other night to last me for a while."

"Let's go to my apartment, then," she said. "I'll make some coffee."

I drove us there. She lived in a small apartment near the university. It had bare wooden floors and peeling plaster on the ceiling. It was an incongruous surrounding for someone who seemed to take such care with her outward appearance. While she was in the kitchen I put a traffic record on a stereo that had only one speaker working. I sat down on a combination sofa and bed and lit a cigarette.

Muffy came out of the kitchen carrying two mugs that were cracked and stained like half-price eggs. "It's not much, is it, Peter?" she said.

"It's about the same as where I live," I said.

"That's what I mean," she said. "But I'm used to it by now." She sat down in a chair that had stuffing peeking out of the Naugahyde covering. "The last two years in New York I lived in a loft that made this place look homey. Of course it didn't help that I threw all the coffee cups in the house at my boyfriend's head just before I left."

"Why did you do that?"

"You know anything about theater, Peter?"

"Some, why?"

"Look, Ted wasn't only a playwright; he was an actor, too. And when an actor gets into a role, it's difficult to get out of. And when you're supposed to be having an affair on stage, it's difficult not to be doing it in real life, too." She sipped at her coffee, winced, and continued. "You've heard it a million times before: leading lady runs off with leading man. I mean, I knew he was boinking other chicks; sometimes he even moved out of the house when he had a part. But one day I went to visit him on a set just to be nice, you know. Someone told me he was going over some of his lines in one of the offices, so I walked down the hall and opened the door to find him getting a blowjob from some bimbo. I mean, this was someone that only had a bit part. That was it; I split."

"And you haven't found anyone else?"

"In this city? You're even more fucked up than I thought you were. Except for that night in the Foam Dome I haven't even bothered to go out of this fucking apartment.''

"Why come to Tallahassee, then, if it's such a drag?''

"My parents live here now.''

"So what?''

"So, look. Everybody's got to have *some* stability. They give me a little money every month until I get my degree.''

"In poetry?''

"Sure.''

"Your parents are rich?''

"*You'd* probably think so. Listen, I hate coffee. Can we go out and get some Jack Daniels or something?''

"Does talking about your parents make you uncomfortable?''

"Talking makes me uncomfortable. Look, are we going to go or what?''

"Let's go.'' I said, getting up. "There's a Jax Liquors down the block from where I live.''

We went out to my car and got in. I drove quickly, without speaking, wondering if I'd be able to make it with her that night. Muffy, too, was mostly silent, and I was wishing I could read her mind. We had a few drinks straight from the bottle as I drove back, but when we got back to her apartment, we nearly bumped into a young woman with blonde ringlets who was coming out one of the other doors of the apartment building.

"Hey,'' Muffy said. "What's up?''

"Nothing. Thought I'd go out somewhere and get a beer.''

"We've got something better than that,'' Muffy said. "Come on inside and I'll make us some drinks.''

Muffy took the bottle into the kitchen while the woman, whose name I never found out, sat down on one side of the sofa bed. I took the Naugahyde chair. Irritated at the woman's presence, I turned the Traffic record back on as Muffy returned with the same two mugs that had held the coffee, plus a plastic Coke cup that she had gotten free with a McDonald's purchase sometime in the distant past. She gave the woman the plastic cup, sat down next to her on the sofa bed, and began making small talk.

I sat quietly and tried to figure out what was going on. First

Muffy had asked me over to her house, now she was using her friend as an excuse to ignore me. Studiously. I was perturbed, but at least it gave me an opportunity to drink and figure my chances.

As it happened, Muffy was very pretty that night. Her hair shimmered down her shoulders, and she was wearing a silver chain that caught the light just enough to give her face a diamond sparkle. The problem was that I didn't think it would be pleasant to hold her. There was an awkward boniness to her shoulders, and her hips looked unmanageable. I was also put off by her mouth—never had I seen more unkissable lips, thin and hard. Although I *wanted* to kiss her very much, there was no way I could see myself doing it. It would be like putting my lips to a manikin or a lamppost. Fascinated at the unkissability, I watched the lips until they were the only part of her I saw—moving lips on an extremely warm spring night. I became drugged by the lips, by her whole mouth, by the words coming from her, nonstop, unhesitating, each one extremely to the point, elucidating, emotional, and revealing. The more I drank, the worse it became. My own mouth was starting to harden, and I knew that unless I stopped drinking I was going to have to arrest those lips by putting my own up against them, and I feared the resulting clank.

I watched politely for about an hour, but it was frustrating. The lips were still there, moving. I wanted to put them in a jar, but Whitey wouldn't leave, didn't dream I wanted her to leave.

Muffy was talking. "My cousin goes to Iowa and she says that in Iowa City things are really incredibly progressive."

"I've never been to Iowa," said Whitey. "It would be cool to drive up there."

"Far out," Muffy said. "But there's just one thing. My cousin's gay."

"A lot of people are."

"Yeah, but I had this incredibly weird dream about Barb trying to seduce me."

"You think she's really going to try something like that?"

"I don't know. It's really weird. I like her and all that—she's an incredibly good person, extremely brilliant—but gay women make me uncomfortable."

"Oh, come on Muffy, let's drive up there."

"I'll have to get some money," Muffy said, "But maybe my parents will spring for it."

She's going to leave me, I thought; before we even like each other she's going to leave me. I was sad about this and I suddenly stood up and moved toward the door. The second side of *The Low Spark of High-Heeled Boys* was playing for the fifth or sixth time and I didn't want to sit through it again now that my chance at capturing Muffy's lips was being taken away.

I slipped out the door without saying goodbye, drove straight to the Foam Dome and ordered a beer. In the pool room a game was being played for small stakes by paddycake players so I carried my beer next door to the Rumpus Room, which had only lately been converted into a bar. Three months before it had been a porno movie house. I sat for a minute on one of a row of folding cinema seats along the wall and listened to the band. I heard only one song before I saw my old girlfriend again, dancing in the corner. For all I knew, she had been bobbing there all week.

I finished my beer quickly and drove home. I was pissed at my old girlfriend, but I was even more pissed at Muffy, who had forced me out of her house and into the bar. I wondered what would have happened if Whitey hadn't shown up.

In my kitchen I warmed up the rest of a pan of hamburger and vegetables I'd cooked for dinner the night before, and put them on a plate. I'd just put the plate on the table and sat down to it when I heard footsteps on the porch, then a knock on the door. I was puzzled. It was after midnight. I looked out and saw a woman's silhouette. I assumed it was one of my neighbors asking to use the phone. It had happened before and I wasn't in the mood.

"My phone's out of order!" I shouted, but the woman stayed at the door. Furious at being bothered so late, I strode to the door, but when I opened it I saw that it was not a neighbor at all; it was Muffy.

For a moment we looked at each other in absolute stillness. I had been thinking about her strongly and now she had appeared like a wish. She stood, waiflike, in the doorway and I just stood there and looked at her, without a greeting and without expression. I had gotten into a habit of coldness and sarcasm after only two long conversations with her, and I was hooked. She walked in and closed the door.

"A normal, well-brought-up person would have asked me in," she said.

"Probably," I agreed.

"I had to walk all the way here and I'm falling down drunk and all you can do is stand there and look at me like you don't even know who I am. Why did you leave, anyway?"

"I seemed superfluous."

"Bullshit. You were the center of attention. You just wanted me to walk four miles."

"It's more like four blocks."

"And I told you that I wasn't into athletics. Are you eating that stuff or is that for the cat?"

"I'm finished," I said. "Why don't you sit down?"

"Don't bother me," she said, walking around like a suspicious home buyer. I followed her.

"What happened to your friend?" I asked.

"Who? I don't have any friends. Is this your bedroom?"

"Yes."

"I have a headache. I have to lie down for a minute, do you mind?"

"No."

"And can you turn off that overhead light? It's getting in my eyes."

I flipped off the switch and lay down next to her on the bed. She rolled next to me, put her head on my shoulder and her leg around my knee. I turned and held her. Her body was hard, lithe, almost rubbery; but it was dark and I couldn't see her lips. I tried to kiss her, but she presented only a slightly puckered mouth, closed fast, and withdrawn almost immediately. "I don't like to kiss," she said. The problem was solved.

I had better luck with her neck and, after our clothes were gone, her breasts. She liked me to stroke her body, but I had a hard time figuring out what else she liked. When I tried to enter her she pushed me away.

"I don't know you well enough," she said. But when I rolled away she pounced on me and rode me sitting up. She took me on a tour of parts of the bed I had never seen, moaning and throwing back her head so far that her hair swept the sheets. She gripped my arms and my chest like she never wanted to let go. I was flattered.

"Come, damn you!" she screamed.

"I don't want to."

"What's wrong with you? Do you have a problem?"

"I don't want to spoil the party."

"Well, look, I'm starting to hurt."

So I came, and we went to sleep. When we woke, we did it again and she moaned in my ear so ecstatically that I finished almost at once.

"You like that, huh?" she said.

"You sounded like you were having a good time, so yes."

"It was fake," she said pointedly, and smiled.

Well, they say that no one's perfect.

*   *   *   *   *

In her apartment a week later, she said, "I steal things."

"What?"

"From department stores."

"Why?" I asked. After only a few days with Muffy I had fallen into the role of brick wall, a state that consists of me sitting and listening, prompting and nodding. It was a role I was familiar with.

She was sitting in the Naugahyde chair. I sat on the sofa bed across the room.

"I *know*. It's horrible, but I have to. My parents don't give me enough to keep me in Corn Flakes. You don't realize it maybe, but I'm a very sophisticated dresser. I'm not used to wearing this Goodwill throwaway shit I have on. In New York when I was living with Ted I was writing copy for an ad agency. I was great at it and they paid me enough to buy anything I wanted.

Now I hardly have enough money to buy cigarettes. Anything else I need—peanut butter, perfume—all disappears into the old handbag."

"It's your life," I said, lighting one of her Marlboros.

"I know. I freak myself out when I think of the risks I'm taking. I mean *freak myself out*. It's just so boring here I have to do crazy things to keep awake. Isn't that awful, Peter? I have to use my creativity just to keep from going *insane*. I don't have anyone to talk to here. I have *no, zero* friends here. *Not one.*"

"You have me."

"And that's really scraping the bottom of the barrel, let me tell you, Peter."

"You don't have to say things like that."

"Look, Peter. You're not a bad guy. The first time you came over I really liked talking to you. Maybe I still do, but I don't think in any normal circumstances I'd want you to come over and visit. Like, I'd do stuff for you for you this week—cook you a dinner, lend you money, anything like that, you know—but I can't see us even being on speaking terms in another month. I mean, I'm not getting anything out of this. You have nothing to offer. *Nothing.* I'm sorry if that sounds unkind, but it's probably better to bring that out in the open."

"I think I'm doing you a lot of good," I said.

"Of course you think that, you're a man. But you're fooling yourself. You're like a cartoonist's version of a psychiatrist."

"And in New York, you had real psychiatrists."

"My mother's a psychiatrist, so I don't need shit from anyone in New York or from you either."

"Still, though, you need me."

"I just want to be left alone."

I got up and put my arms around her.

"What are you doing?" she asked.

"I'm going to fuck you."

"You mean *you* are going to make a move on *me* for a change?"

I picked her up and carried her to the bedroom. As I was taking off her clothes she was still talking.

"I can't believe you, Peter. I hit you with the vilest, most cutting putdowns ever and you get *excited*. Ohhh.''

"I want you to sit on me in front of the mirror so I can watch."

"You're really perverted, you know that?"

"Shut up," I said.

She sank down on me and gasped. "In, out. In, out. How boring. The same old thing over and over. There must be something else. I need some originality."

"It beats touching yourself," I said.

"Masturbating is boring, too," she hissed. "But I suppose I'll have to do it when you finish."

"You know the real reason I don't like you, Peter?" she said later.

I didn't answer. I could think of a number of reasons.

"Because you can't give me any real pain."

"Is that what you want?"

"It's either that or happiness, and I've left the only man who could ever give me that. I want real pain. I want to be emotionally crushed. . . ."

"You want to fall in love," I told her.

"I suppose."

*   *   *   *   *

There's nothing like a relationship—even a sick one—to take your mind off your troubles. For almost two weeks I avoided the bars and rarely thought about my old girlfriend. I felt needed for the first time in more than a year—needed in a vague, impossible-to-put-into-words way—and I was trying hard to make it work. I sometimes thought that Muffy needed me only to vent her sarcasm on, and it made me feel uncomfortable and used. But it couldn't make me feel as bad as having no one at all. If she wanted to rant at me, okay. I was getting sex, of a sort, and companionship, also of a sort. No one else had ever thought I was quite so much of an asshole, but I tried not to pay too much attention to the things she said about me. I was the only one she had, after all.

One afternoon I finally lured her out to the tennis court and found out that she was a better player than she pretended, although badly out of condition. The courts were in a secluded part of town, surrounded by acres of trees. It was a warm day and the running and the sweating were stimulating. When we finished, there was a light in her eyes I had not seen before. It was exhilaration and lust all at once.

"God, Peter, I feel like an animal."

"You want to go into the woods?"

"Let's go."

Things were looking up.

A few days later she said she wanted to swim and lie on the beach, so I rented a motel room for the two of us in Panama City. I saw a chance of stabilizing the relationship, hoping we'd be drawn together by being totally alone in a strange city; by having a clean, cool, neutral place to stay.

Instead, I had a flat tire halfway there.

She had been enjoying the ride, watching the pines lining the long flowing open road, the rises, the expanses of beach viewed through the uncleared approaches. She had her head on my shoulder when the plies on the tire separated. It sounded like a helicopter was hovering a foot overhead. I stopped the car.

"My spare is flat, too," I said.

"Wonderful."

My lips were pressed together so hard they were a line on my face. We had passed no gas stations for miles and most of the ones we passed before that had looked deserted. It was 4:00 in the afternoon and very hot. A flat tire (an impersonal, unemotional piece of bad luck) was bad enough, but my lack of foresight concerning the spare made it far worse. It was the first stupid thing I'd done in Muffy's presence, and I began throwing my arms around in disgust. "Shit," I said. "Fuck! I hate shit like this to happen."

She tried to calm me down, but I didn't want to calm down. I saw some kind of store up ahead and I started walking toward it. Muffy went across the street to what looked like a cheap motel. The store people told me there was a gas station over the next rise, about a mile away. I went back to tell Muffy.

"What's wrong with the spare?" she asked.

"Slow leak. I took it off a week ago."

"Will it hold air?"

"Maybe for a day."

"There's a kid in the motel who has a compressor air pump."

"Let's get it."

I rolled the tire over and the kid pumped it up. The tire held.

It was dark when we got into Panama City. I bought another tire at a K-Mart, but it was a busy time and we had to wait for over an hour for the tire to be mounted. I was hot, smelly, dirty, and very irritable. Muffy had seen me out of control and I resented it. Along with that came further resentment for all the past misery she'd given me—bad feelings I had tried to ignore.

Dinner calmed me only slightly, and in the motel room I grabbed Muffy and started taking her clothes off, although she didn't want me to.

"Don't," she said.

"Why?"

"You're hurting me."

"I thought that's what you wanted."

"What?"

"I thought you wanted to be hurt."

"It does hurt, and I don't want it."

By now I was moving inside her and a sense of duty or hidden affection was causing her to try and stay with me. But I was still way too emotional and I lasted only a minute or two.

I rolled off her and smoked a cigarette, feeling like the worst prick that ever lived and way too much of a prick to admit it. Muffy lay silent. The expression on her face, almost mockingly indifferent, gave me the sudden realization that, in many respects, it had been no different for her this time than it had ever been, and that thought made me furious all over again. In a calm voice, I said, "That was the worst fuck we've ever had."

"What?"

"You heard me."

"Well, what do you want from me? You can't just fuck somebody anytime you want to. I hurt. What can I do?"

"You could try and let me give you a little pleasure for a

change."

"Look, I told you. I can't come that way."

"You don't open up enough. Your mind is closed. You don't want me to give you pleasure."

"I don't want you to give me anything," she said.

"Enough said." I rolled over on my stomach and faced away from her.

"I don't know why you're mad."

"I'm not mad."

"Is that why you won't look at me? Is that why you tell me I'm the worst fuck you've ever had?"

I didn't answer.

"This is weird," she said. I heard her cross to the other bed and lie down. "This is really something."

I reached up and turned out the light.

"So you're just going to go to sleep?" she asked.

"Um hmm."

"You've really got a problem."

I didn't answer. She rolled over in the other bed.

"I can't stand it," she said. "What are you trying to do to me?"

"I just don't feel like talking."

"Do you mind if I scream?"

"If that's what your mother would advise."

She was silent for a long time, but I heard her tossing around on the bed. Finally she said, "Look, I hate this." She paused, then went on. "Let me explain something to you. I told you that my mother was a psychiatrist, but I didn't mention that she is one of the most brilliant women alive. Her IQ isn't even on the chart, and my father is no slouch either. Well, how would you like it if you were an only daughter and your parents, who have studied all their lives to be the best, expect you to be better? How would you like to have ten questions when you come home every day about what you've learned in school? *Every day*? And don't get me wrong, my parents hate each other. My future as a genius was the only thing they ever agreed on. It took twenty years for me to fall in love despite them, and when I did, I cut myself off from them like a rotten limb on the family tree."

"You don't have to go into all this," I said softly.

"You've made me go into it. I staked my whole life on my relationship with Ted, and three years later I find out that I was wrong. The only thing in my life that I ever wanted and I find out that it was wrong. Well, what am I supposed to do now? Where can I go from here? Back to my parents? Do you know how hard it is for me to even live in the same *town* with them? I can only take so much extracurricular shit. Do you see why I'm scared to get into situations like this one with you? If it turns out bad it'll push me over my shit threshold and I'll have to leave town, and *then* what'll I do?"

Muffy paused, and I thought I heard her catch her breath in a sob. "Thanks for taking advantage of me," she said. "Thanks for trapping me here."

"I'm sorry," I said, and I meant it.

"Forget it," she said. After a few moments of silence she said, "I'm not going to be able to sleep." She got up and came over to my bed and got in behind me. "Can I lie next to you as long as I'm going to be awake all night? Do you mind?"

I turned over and touched her. There were tears on her cheeks. "Put your arms around me," I said. She did. We held each other and she kissed me for the first time. I stroked her until she came. That, too, was the first time. We slept close.

In the morning she was businesslike. The beach was beautiful and the sun was hot. There were too many people but I tried to ignore them. As the day passed, Muffy and I became distant. We were both thinking of the night before.

Lying on the sand, I watched Muffy swimming with strong, confident strokes. She was one of the most self-reliant people I knew, and one of the most careful. She had given in to a whim and now was trapped in a strange city with no friends and no car. For just one day I had taken away her power, and she hated it. I did too.

I tried to make it up to her. On the drive home I began playing a role. I pretended I was in love with her. This confused her because she was trying to make me hate her. I became very tender and dramatic, even silly. "Do you think my hair is getting too thin?" I asked casually.

"You're nuts," she answered, incredulous. "Why would you ask me something like that? What do I care about your fucking hair? Who are you, anyway?"

And those elusive lips. I really grew to love them. When we were nearly home I stopped at a light, leaned over, and kissed her. It was completely unexpected, this lover's gesture, because we had been coldly silent to each other for almost an hour. She blushed and turned her head away in confusion—the only shy expression she ever showed me. She said softly, almost demurely, "What are you doing? Leave me alone."

Still, it was the nicest moment.

After that, we saw each other less. Our fights became more bitterly sarcastic, more openly cruel, but she still suffered me to come around because she was lonely and had no other friends.

"You're really an incredibly thick person, Peter," she told me on one of my weekly visits. "When I think of the men I could have had in Boston one summer . . ."

"Go back and get them."

"I will when I'm ready."

"When will that be?"

"When I'm a good enough poet."

"You've been doing pretty well lately."

"You're not much of a critic, you know that?"

"Some people think I am."

"Some people think that poems about tennis are okay, too," she said. "But that's because you're limited; you're a very limited person. You've lived in Florida too long. It's really not your fault. You didn't have the right teachers and your parents are probably fucked up. Don't get mad at that. I'm a wreck thinking about *my* family. But I've lived through it so far and I'm trying to live through some more. That's why I can't go back to New York yet. I've got to accept all the horrible, shitty, incredibly insane goings on I've had to deal with all my life. Peter, I'm only twenty-three years old and I feel like I'm starting my third life."

"You've got a lot to work with."

"I know."

"You think too much about thinking. How long is it going to take you to forget about those New York and Boston jerks so you can live and react like a human? You're like a snapshot cut into little pieces."

"Well look, Peter, I don't appreciate you coming in here and telling me I'm the most untogether person you know. I don't like you telling me how to act or what to do. I don't like it at all, and if you think that way, why don't you leave? Why don't you leave right now?"

"I'll leave when I'm ready."

"Well then, do. I'm not going to fight with you, but don't mind me if I ignore you."

"Look," I began. "I've done stupid things around you and I'm sorry, but you're under a wrong impression. I don't love you. You can't crush me and I don't want to crush you even if I could. You dwell on your own pain and ignore mine. You talk about your ex-love and completely ignore the fact that I might be unhappy too. You've never asked me a single question about myself. You're not the only fucked up person on the planet. You were supposed to be a cathartic, not another sore. If you don't want to be nice to me, then fuck you. If I want real pain I can just go back to what I was doing before I met you."

For a few seconds she had no words to respond. Then she said, "I don't need your problems," but her words were soft. She picked up her tennis racquet from the floor and turned it over in her hands. She looked demure, waiflike. I remembered how she had looked when she first came to my house, two months before. I remembered how she had looked after our tennis match, and I decided to make a last attempt.

"Do you think you might like to play tennis sometime?" I asked.

She was caught off guard. "I don't know." Maybe she was thinking the same thing I was: the heat, the action, the woods. "Probably not."

I smiled. "Well, then," I said, "I'll see you around."

She looked at me seriously and nodded. I closed the door behind me.

I drove straight to the Rumpus Room and sat down in one of the old porno house seats. My old friend was there dancing with drunks. Her hair looked a bit wetter, her body a bit more fleshy. Her eyes were still closed. I got a beer and watched her. I lit a cigarette.

I felt real pain.

The Sexless Ones

The air is thick in this bar. I feel like I'm swimming in a bottle of perfume. Other people dance, but I don't. I stand against a wall, watching faces spin around. The lights are like busy night traffic. The dancers are frenetic shoppers. I have a hollow in my belly that wants to suck the rest of me inside.

*　　*　　*　　*　　*

Saturday nights are the worst. Other nights you have a job to worry about, or you worry about sleep. Even on Fridays you try to convince yourself that you are tired from your job, but of course you aren't. You tell yourself that you can sit home and rest, but of course you can't. The hollow threatens to buoy you up and float you out the window and into the street. A can of beer weighs you down almost enough. Four beers and you've gotten through another Friday with only yourself for company. On Saturdays you can't do that. Saturdays weigh more. Saturdays vomit you and your four beers up and spill you through streets you are familiar with only in daylight. Neon signs are blurred, cars honk out personal insults at you alone, the streets themselves become narrower. No faces (and you search continuously) are familiar. It's as if you've seen and done nothing before. You are born every Saturday at dusk. You die then, too.

*　　*　　*　　*　　*

I walk out of the perfume a watery blur. Unseen, I follow two disco queens into the parking lot. They have short hair, short dresses, and black polish on their fingers and toes. As I open my car door, a small dog yaps at me but I kick it away. I let the taillights of the disco queens lure me. I am the trailing end of their beam of light. We are connected by a filament, by something precarious. The streets are rabid. They always are on Saturday night. But I have fish instincts. I know how to swerve when swerving is called for.

* * * * *

We are at City of Night, another disco. I smoke cigarettes, one after another, to warm the air I breathe. I blow smoke at men in the bar, but they are queers and think I am just being coy. In fact, this is a queer hangout and I realize that the disco queens are fag hags. I loathe them now. I loathe everything.

"Give me a beer!" I shout.

"Let *me* buy," says a voice at my ear. A thin black man in his late thirties is at my elbow. His shirt was woven by one thousand black spiders and his single earring is a skull.

"Forget it," I say. I look over the dance floor like a man viewing his last sight from a scaffold. The music is like blood pounding through my ears.

"I seen you around," says the voice.

"Beat it!"

"I seen you, because I do the same things you do."

"What things?"

"I stand around and watch."

"You're crazy."

"I seen you *here* before," the black man says. I am pouring beer down my throat.

"I've never been here before," I say.

"You were here last Saturday, and the Saturday before that." The man has a gold tooth that gleams like a facet in the round, spinning mirrors above.

"You're wrong."

"You follow the women. . . ."

"What about it?"

"But you never talk to them."

"They're all bitches!"

"All of them?"

"All of them who come here."

"You should give it up," he says.

"Give what up?"

"All this." His hand sweeps around the room like the second hand on a clock. I follow it with my eyes. Everything I see disgusts me. The man is looking at my pants hard enough to burn a hole through the fabric.

*   *   *   *   *

So you get in your car again, when you find it, and careen madly through town. You are looking for other bars, for sexual adventures with women whose chests jut out obscenely. But you know no women. Even the ones you have worshipped from afar have disappeared. Other cars are screaming at you now, but this can be ignored. At a light, a black limosine lingers. The street is jiving with blacks. Loud music blares from store windows. Blacks stand around in groups like the big bunches of purple grapes on faded posters ripping from the wooden store fronts. Beer bottles and crumpled wads of paper lie about like dead mice.

You want to speed up to the beat of your rushing blood but the car ahead of you is going 3 mph. You shout at the top of your lungs, "Mother fuck!" but that does you no good. Black faces turn to grin and leer at you. Someone throws a pop bottle that crashes off your hood. The limosine stops and you are trapped. The other lane is filled with the mob of people who have chosen you as their excitement. Rocks and whirling glasses are flying at you from all directions and you continue to scream out, "Motherfucking asslicking dicksuckers!"

A man brandishes a broken whiskey bottle inches from your rolled-up window. "Asslickah?" he grins. "Mutha *fuck*ah?"

You hold your head up and stare into the deep brown of the man's eyes. Other eyes peer at you from the back of the limosine.

"We gone cut your balls off!" The mob swarms around your car, thicker than darkness.

*   *   *   *   *

In the limosine, I am sitting next to the black man with the skull earring. "You run away too fast," he says. Beside him sits the blackest dog I've ever seen. So black it looks like a shadow on the darkest night. I see only the glint of razor teeth. In the front seat sit two men almost as black as the dog. One drives, the other looks back at me. In one hand he holds a knife, in the other he has money.

I would vomit if I could, but my sickness goes beyond that. My hollowness is filled with a fear that tastes green and fetid. The man with the skull earring puts a hand on my knee. "You're a precipitous man," he tells me.

"I meant what I said," I say.

"Motherfuck?" he says. "Asslick?"

"Yes!"

"And dick suck?"

The dog growls and gnashes its teeth.

"Give it up," the man says.

"I don't want to hear it," I tell him.

"Why? Just look at Haze. He has to give it up too—that money, his knives. He live too fast. And he who live too fast never be living at all."

"I'd rather die, man," says the man called Haze.

"Yes," says the man next to me. He turns my way again. "Maude is a Belgian Shepherd. She is specially trained."

The man called Haze looks fearfully back at the dog and grips his knife tighter.

"See there, Haze is already learning to choose. But choosing ain't enough. He can't kill his own fear with that knife, and he can't buy it off. Watch." The man sees Haze prying at the door handle. "Maude! Jump!" At this command the dog flies over the seat like a streak of black light. A horrible wail comes from Haze's lips. His hands are thrown into the air; money is fluttering and the knife is stuck through the top of the limosine.

"That's fear," says the man beside me. I peer over the seat and past the moaning, trembling, sweating Haze. The dog is between his legs, her mouth open over his crotch. She growls and drips saliva on his sequined pants.

"Don't, man," he wails. "Don't."

"That is Maude's one trick," says the man beside me. "She can bite off the dick and balls of any man alive in less time than it takes to chop off a finger. Does it scare you?"

"Any man would be afraid."

"Any man, yes."

"You're scared yourself," I say.

"Ha. And you are too drunk to think."

"Maybe so," I answer. Excitement tortures me and I open my mouth to let some of the pressure out of my body. Nothing happens.

The driver stops the car in front of a row of slatboard apartments. He looks at Haze, who has fainted on the seat. He snickers in a high, whinnying voice.

"This is my apartment," says the man with the skull earring. "Come in."

"Said the spider to the fly," I say.

The man laughs. "Maybe you're not too drunk after all." His tooth glints like a cache of ore in a dark tunnel. "Come, Maude."

*   *   *   *   *

The peeling walls are covered with pictures of men and women. Some of them you have seen at different times and different places. You recognize a drag queen, now dressed in a shirt and tie; there is a woman you once worshipped who suddenly stopped party-going. The man with the gold tooth is there; his driver is too.

You find yourself drinking again. The ceiling is so high you're not sure it's there at all. Sirens outside are blaring like the racing blood that has been spurting through your ears all night, but amplified. The sound fills much of the hollowness that is left, but then it recedes and half of you seeks to fly through the roof and explode outward on the city, to splatter each and every person with a part of your misery. A black dog sits at your feet with hungry eyes. From another room comes a sermon, echoing out like words through deserted halls, or maybe the words are just echoing through your hollowness.

"You think you are handsome? Look on the walls; there are ten handsomer than you. There are ten uglier, too. There are ten better lovers. Ten richer, ten smarter, ten who know how to use guns and sticks. Those are all things you have to give up to become something real. Not a *man*. Not a stud, not a man of property. Look at the pictures on the walls. See the pain in the eyes. It's all there, but it's a pain that's rich and beautiful— not ugly like yours. You still cling to your anger and your stupid bitterness. You got to give all that up."

The voice is suddenly in your ear and you look from the pictures and see the man in a robe and slippers. His chest is black and hairless. His skull earring has been replaced by a heart-shaped one. It and his tooth glint in unison, like twin glimmers of light racing out to embrace each other. Your head tries to roll off your neck but you hold it steady and think that maybe something has been slipped into your drink. No matter. The night is nearly over. Tomorrow you'll stay home in front of the TV. Monday is a work day and you will need rest. The thought of this transcends disgust and despair. Your hollowness will not subside. It is as big as the ocean and it rumbles and crashes in your belly. Beside you, the man has taken off his robe and stands bare.

You reach out to the empty place between his legs and touch only scarred flesh. The man throws his head back and laughs and the laughter fills you like a meal of worms.

"Who are those people?" you ask, as the faces begin popping out of their frames. Your hand has recoiled from the man's flesh to your own, but you are cold and wilted like a frozen vegetable.

"The sexless ones," he says.

And now you know. It hits you with the gentle force of an ejaculation. It sizzles on your skin. It fills you up until you feel pregnant with resolve. The black dog watches closely as you stand, as you loosen your belt, as you slowly give yourself up to her waiting jaws.

The pain is as sweet as death, but richer and more beautiful.

Nameless

I was starting to go to the dogs.

I don't know; some people said the whole town was going to the dogs when they legalized parimutuel betting back in 1968. Before that, the only money that ever changed hands around here via wager was a buck or two at the old stock car races. Back then the track was dirt and the bleachers were rickety, but every Saturday afternoon a couple of hundred people would get in the family station wagon and spend the day with peanuts, beer, and sunshine. Nobody ever won more than a couple of dollars at these races, but nobody ever lost much either. I used to drive in a race every once in a while, but because that's where this story ends up, I'll begin again.

I was on my way to the dog races with my friend John Biggeorge, and I was determined to go every night until I succeeded in losing all the money that Jasper Quincy Honkerton—a man I'd never even heard of—had left me in his will.

"What else can you do with a hundred thousand dollars?" I asked Biggeorge in the doorway of his junk shop.

My friend thought awhile, shrugged, pulled on a blue Air Force jacket with the stripes torn off, and locked up for the evening. "I'm glad my mother died," he said as he opened the door of my black and red '57 Buick and got in, settling back amid the sliced and hanging seat covers. He closed the door with a crunch.

"Come again?" I said. I cranked up the car and revved the engine.

"Poor. I'm glad she died poor so she couldn't leave me anything." Then he added, "I hate money."

"How do you know?" I asked. "You've never had any."

"I mean I hate the color of money."

"You hate green?" I asked.

"Yeah." Biggeorge slumped into himself for a minute, then

looked out the window. "And I don't like red too much either."

"I think some of that junk has gotten into your attic," I said.

"Why don't you buy yourself something with some of the money?" he asked. He reached out with a finger and casually scooped dust off the fissured dash. "I mean, couldn't you use a new car? It's for sure that this one will never race again."

"It's not going to have to," I said.

"That doesn't explain why you want to throw away a hundred thousand dollars."

I turned a corner furiously. "I'm not smart enough to have that much money," I said. "If I start spending it, I'll probably want to sell the garage and eat in expensive restaurants and smoke cigars. And I don't even like cigars. And what will I do when the money runs out? Anyway, Honkerton was the one who earned the money; I didn't."

"Hell, the man's dead and he didn't have a relative in the world."

"So?"

"So spend the dough. He's not gonna want it back."

"I wouldn't want a dead man spending *my* money," I retorted.

This seemed sound reasoning to Biggeorge, who scratched the stubble on his round red face and settled back into the fuzz. "Well, I guess you could just give it to charity."

"No way," I said, screeching around another corner. "It's *my* goddam money."

"Why do you always speed up when you turn corners?" asked Biggeorge.

"An old race driver's trick," I answered. It was an easy answer because I had met Biggeorge shortly after I had retired from racing and he would never know the difference anyway.

"I guess the rubber you lay down kind of protects the street, doesn't it?" he asked. "You never told me why you gave up racing."

"I retired after a big win," I said. "I wanted to go out with a bang."

"Really? Did you win much money?" he asked.

"Minus twenty-five dollars and two days in jail."

"That doesn't sound like a whole lot," he said. "What did they put you in jail for?"

"Speeding," I replied.

"Speeding?" Biggeorge asked in disbelief.

"Speeding," said the cop thirty seconds later. "You seemed to be accelerating around that last corner at about 45. How about lettin me see your license."

I took out my faded and roach-eaten wallet, carefully removed the license, and handed it to the cop.

The cop shone a flashlight on the picture. "Brooks, eh? Used to have a pretty heavy beard there, didn't you, Brooks?"

"It comes and goes," I said.

The cop looked at me as if to see if I was trying to get wise, then did a slight double take. "Haven't I seen you somewhere before?" he asked.

"Well, I've been around," I answered, moving my head farther into the shadowy interior of the car.

The cop starting writing out a ticket. "What I'm giving you is a summons to appear in Municipal Court on the 15th. Do you realize what would happen if everybody speeded?" he asked.

"You'd have to give tickets to people for going too slow?" I asked.

The cop smiled and wrote a couple more lines. "I didn't see your right turn indicator flashing around that corner," he said. "And that muffler should be muffled before the next time you drive. Can you think of anything else?"

"Not right now."

He handed me the ticket and smiled again. "Have a safe day," he said.

When the cop had gone and we were speeding and sputtering along again, I handed the ticket to Biggeorge and motioned to the glove compartment. "Put it in the GC," I told him.

Biggeorge looked at the ticket in the dim light of the dash. "Twenty-five bucks," he said. "Say, where did you get a license that says Buster B. Brooks? I thought you didn't have a name."

I gritted my teeth and steered wildly around a taxi, narrowly missing it. "I don't," I answered. "Brooks brought his car in

for servicing a month or so ago and left his license in the car.
I took it."

"Why?"

"The one I had that said Peter Quirk had expired."

"And how did you get *it*?"

"Same way. You find a lot of things in people's cars."

"Why don't you get your own license?"

"Oh, you know," I said.

"No, why? It seems like it'd make things a lot easier for you."

We were driving through town now and the highway was dotted
with streetlights, identical and evenly spaced. "The Bureau of
Motor Vehicles won't give me one unless I change my name,"
I told him.

"Change my name?" I had asked the matronly woman with
fancy-rimmed spectacles who wore a flowery print dress, had her
hair in a bun, and sat behind the desk at the Bureau. The room
had smelled like an air conditioned pencil sharpener. "Why should
I have to change my name?"

"So we can put it on the license," she told me.

"But my name's already on the license," I said.

"You forget that we haven't made you a license yet," she said.

I pointed to a form in front of her on the desk. "But it would
go on that blank line, right?" I persisted.

"Yes."

"That blank line *is* my name," I said.

"A blank line isn't a name," she said, trying not to get testy.

"Not only is it a name, as I've already shown you on my birth
certificate, but I think it'll catch on. Even now think of all the
unborn babies in the world that are named for me."

"Children who aren't born yet don't have . . ." Her voice
trailed off as her gaze drifted toward the ceiling.

"Har har," I said.

"Perhaps you'd better . . ."

"Probably, but say I *did* decide to change my name. What
would I have to do?"

"The first thing would be to go down to the courthouse and
fill out a petition for a name change."

"What's that, a form of some kind?"

"That's right."

"You're talking about a blank form, right? One that I'd have to sign?" I asked.

"Of course."

"How would I sign it?" I asked.

"What?" She was confused again.

"What makes you think that the courthouse would accept my signature when you won't?"

"Oh, hell," she sighed. So did Biggeorge. "Oh hell, I wish I had all these tickets," he said as he took out a huge pile of the white slips from the glove compartment.

"You what?" I asked.

"I mean I wish I had a dollar for every ticket you have here."

"Don't mess them up," I told him. "They're in order. Just put the latest one on top."

Biggeorge thumbed incredulously through the assortment of summonses. "There must be at least fifty in here. Don't you ever get tired of paying for these things?"

"I don't pay," I told him. "I just collect them."

"They'll put your kazoongie in the calaboose." he said.

"They'll put Buster B. Brooks' kazoongie in the calaboose. In fact, I think Peter Quirk may be there right now."

"What for?"

"Driving with an expired license."

"Not bad," Biggeorge said admiringly. "But speaking of licenses, that cop took the number of your license plate. Can't they trace you through that?"

"I've got sway with the junkyard dealers. They give me licenses from wrecks or cars that blow up on the highway."

"Maybe I could sell some of those in my shop?" he mused.

"They'd put your kazoongie in the calaboose."

"I suppose," he said.

The night was huge and unclouded. All around us were the moving lights of automobiles and the sounds of a moving city. With another sigh, Biggeorge settled back and watched the lights zip by going the other way. Signs advertising The Dawn Club,

The Miramir, and Cafe Electric flashed their messages through the car's windows. The buildings were drab and run down. A few people could be seen walking on the sidewalks in both directions. Most were drunk already or well on their way.

I steered the car into a well-lit parking lot just beyond the limit of the downtown area and pulled into a parking space well away from the huge building that was the race track clubhouse. Biggeorge and I got out, walked the distance to the building, and paid fifty cents to enter. Another quarter got us a racing form. In and around the tiers of seats, hundreds of other people were already milling about and expressing discontent at one thing or another in low voices. A loudspeaker was blaring all sorts of nonsense through the highly acoustical and cigar-smelly room.

We had almost made it to the ticket window when a hand slapped me on the back with a whap. "Hey Nameless, hawaya boy? I haven't seen ya in ages." This came from a dapper and smiling man with a thin mustache and brown, well-tailored suit. "And how are *you*, Big Gawrge?"

"Mouse Man," I sighed, resigned to a bad few minutes. Mouse Man was a lawyer and the executor of Jasper Quincy Honkerton's estate.

"The very same," he said.

I got in the shortest of the ticket lines with Biggeorge. Biggeorge nodded to Mouse Man and went to studying his program.

"My name's not Nameless," I said.

"So you say," he said. "But you could always change it to Nameless; I mean, if you liked that name."

"I don't." I was looking at Mouse Man's well-tailored crotch, wondering which side would best receive a well-placed kick. I knew a guy who had tried that once, but missed.

"I knew a guy once who tried that," said Mouse Man.

"Tried what?" asked Biggeorge.

"Changing his name. It worked out good for him, too."

"How's that?"

"Guy's name was Appleblossom, but he wanted to run for city council against this black guy named Higgenbottom. He didn't think anybody'd want to vote for anybody named Appleblossom, so he changed his name to George Washington. Now Appleblossom was a real dork and everybody knew it, but in a low-key campaign, people tend to forget names. All they knew was that they wanted to vote for the black guy."

"And Washington is a black name, so . . ." I began.

"That's right," Mouse Man giggled. "They all voted for Appleblossom by mistake."

I looked at his crotch longingly, but refrained.

Biggeorge was next in line. He leaned over and whispered to Mouse Man, "Number seven in the first."

"Thanks Big Gawrge," said Mouse Man. He put his hands deep into his pockets, as if to ward off kicks to the privates, and shuffled quickly into another line.

After I had placed my own bet, I walked over to where Biggeorge was lounging and asked, "What did you go and give a tip to Mouse Man for? That's not like you."

"Did it because Mouse Man's a kazoongie."

"But you told him to bet on number seven in the first race."

"Number seven has scratched from the first race," he said.

"That *is* like you."

We bustled our way through the crowd and outside to where the bleachers overlooked the track. A ring of lights on poles circled the inside of the track, illuminating things so brightly and clearly that I could see the dust puff up from the handlers' sneakers as they walked their dogs into the starting gates.

"Who'd you bet on?" Biggeorge asked.

"Don't know."

"How could you not know who you bet on?"

"I tore out the names of the dogs from my program, then picked one name at random and showed it to the ticket seller. I put a hundred bucks on it to win."

"What happens if it *does* win?"

"Then I collect."

"Why not just throw your tickets away now and assume you lost? Then maybe later I can mosey back here, pick them up, and you'll never be the wiser."

"Forget it."

"Why not, what difference will it make?"

"It makes a lot of difference," I used to tell the teachers at school on the first day of classes. You see, they were trying to confuse me with my older brother because of the way our names are spelled. After homeroom or class I usually had to stay and explain the difference at the blackboard. "Our names are pronounced the same," I said to them, but he spells his like this: —————— (I drew a straight line on the board); I don't spell mine at all."

"And you call that a lot of difference?" the stubborn teacher would inquire.

The truth is that names weren't something that my father went in for. He thought they were redundant, and often pointed to the fact that "Hey, you," or "Hey, asshole," had exactly the same effect as using a proper name. He also disliked the idea that there were so many people on earth with the same names. Even if someone got creative and came up with something like Gronqx or Pltspk, someone else would probably come right along and copy it.

When my sister was born, my mother remained under sedation for quite a while, and the nurse handed the birth certificate to my father to complete. After briefly toying with the notion of naming my sister You, Asshole, Gronqx, or Pltspk, he simply shook his head and wrote None on the dotted line.

For that reason, my sister was always called None, although when she turned fifteen, she changed the spelling to Nun, which made her more popular with the boys.

A year later, when my brother was born, my father was craftier. Mother still being under ether, he marked the dotted line with a straight line. Much to my father's dismay, my brother always signed his name like this: ————, which was very similar to the signature of many famous people.

I don't mean to intimate that my mother was a party to these names, or lack of same. She was just a very busy woman who rarely used proper names anyway. She simply called people Darling or Sweetheart or some other endearment as she bustled from one engagement to another. Her own name, Matilda, gave her a tendency to agree with my father's choices anyway, although she never admitted it.

In any case, when I came along, my father simply skipped over the dotted line and chortled himself into an early grave. I'm sure that had he lived to see Jasper Quincy Honkerton's legacy, he would have felt a sort of triumph.

After I graduated from high school I took a variety of jobs, none of which were very interesting. I always liked fixing cars, though, so I took a voc-ed course in mechanics, then fixed up an old jalopy I bought in a junkyard. I installed a couple of four barrels under the hood and stuck some racing slicks on the wheels. With decals of orange fire on the outside, I was ready to fly. I got a job in a garage (the same one I ended up buying, years later) and started hanging out at the races. At first, they were pretty informal, so when someone scratched, they might let me fill in. "After all," I used to explain to the officials, "you've already penciled my name into the open slot."

I loved it—the curves, the spins, the screeching of tires. I actually got pretty good at it after a couple of years, although it must have been pretty confusing for the fans until they got used to me.

"Better get used to me," said Biggeorge from my side.

"What?" I asked.

"You better get used to me being poor. My dog just lost by twenty lengths."

I peeked at the number I had selected and breathed a sigh of relief. "Mine, too."

So we just sat there for six races and lost money. In the seventh race Biggeorge actually recouped his losses and a little more when he boxed two longshots that came in. I, on the other hand was a consistent loser. So far I had lost $100 in each race except the seventh, when I lost $400 by betting on all eight dogs to win, with the actual winner paying only 2-1. That was $1,000 down and $99,000 to go.

While Biggeorge and most of the people around us were hunched over their racing forms, I was content to sit back, light a cigar, and watch the dogs being led onto the track. Greyhounds are beautiful animals, but strange—all muscle and skin. They are the waspwaisted, surefooted monarchs of their species. Ex-racecar-driver that I was, I envied them their graceful speed. Not too much, though, because if it weren't for my racing exploits, I would never have been named as Jasper Quincy Honkerton's beneficiary.

Evidently, it happened this way.

Jasper Quincy Honkerton was a semisuccessful manufacturer of trampolines. Although he was in his mid-70s, he had never had an illness more serious than a cold. In fact, he considered himself the epitome of perfect health and not only designed, but often worked out on, his own trampolines. In his study one evening, writing notes about introducing some new resilience into the material he used in his trampolines, he was totally unprepared for the massive heart attack he began to suffer. The pain made him want to cry out, but he could mutter only a croak. Realizing with shocked finality that he had not disposed of his property, he frantically tore a page from his notebook and began to write his last will and testament.

> I, Jasper Q. Honkerton, being of sound mind, do hereby
> bequeath all my worldly possessions to

At this point he collapsed at his desk and died.

His executor was Mouse Man, who being an avid race fan, knew me and assumed that the will was complete. It was he who disposed of Honkerton's holdings and, after pocketing a hefty executor's fee, handed me a check for $100,000.

"I don't want the money," I told him.

"I'll take it, then," he said.

"Forget it."

By the tenth race the track had gotten soft, and small clouds of brown-orange clay billowed out behind the pack of dogs as they ran full out, their muzzles pointing at the rabbit-on-a-stick. I was still doing okay, but hadn't lost nearly as much as I would have liked. As in the first race, the number seven dog had scratched, lowering the odds a bit. That didn't matter much to me, as the two favorites left the gate quickly and steadily outdistanced the pack. They photo-finished almost twenty lengths ahead of the next finisher.

I had bet on the dog that came in last, yet something about that race reminded me of my own last race, not so many years before.

A friend of mine who worked at the race track called me one morning and told me that if I could get to the track in fifteen minutes, I could go into the last row for a car that had blown an engine in warm-ups. Sounds kind of haphazard, but that's how I made my money in those days. The trouble was, I lived on one side of town and the track was on the other.

I grabbed my helmet from the hatrack and was through the first red light almost before I started the car. And it was woe to any driver that didn't get out of my way. Hairy steering and a four-lane highway got me through the busiest section in about ten minutes, although I'd picked up a cop about a mile back who was doggedly trying to get my attention. He did, and I squealed down an alley shortcut and out again into a one-way straightaway. Then I gunned it, damning every single vehicle that was in my way straight to hell.

I looked at my watch and saw that my fifteen minutes were up, but the road I was on led straight to the track now. I could see its oval facade dead ahead. I caught a glimpse of a flashing red light behind me as I turned into the track's parking lot, so I tromped harder on the gas. My wheels were burning too much rubber for me to hear whether the cop was blasting his siren or not. He was too late anyway. I burned around to the back entrance and saw my friend holding the gate open and frantically gesturing me forward.

I blew in the gate, slowing just enough to see what was happening.

The white pace car was about halfway through the starting lap, with five rows of cars bunched behind and waiting for it to get the hell out of the way. Just before the starter could pass in front of the gate, I slammed out in front of him and burned rubber in a zigzag and screeching course down the track. The starter still had a quarter lap to go before it pulled off into the pits to let the cars go. I'd gotten lucky timing; by the time the slowpoke had gotten out of the way, I'd lapped and was right up on the pack, but doing about double their speed. Before any of them had a chance to rev up their motors and change gears, I'd passed them on the outside. By the time anyone else had gained top speed, I was three-quarters of a lap ahead of the next car and slowly edging up on the last car in the pack again. As I passed the gate for the second time I was alone in the lead, taking corners on two wheels and really giving it everything the old jalopy had.

But suddenly I wasn't alone anymore; someone was actually stealing up on me despite my virtual head start. My rearview mirror was filled by a flashing red light. It was the cop. I gunned around the next turn, nearly spinning out into the retaining wall, but the cop did the same and I gained a little. I was searching my mirror for him when I suddenly found myself nearly kissing the last driver in the regular pack. I swerved to the inside, nearly spinning into the pits, but straightened out just in time to negotiate the next car—this time to the outside. I heard a roar go up from the crowd and looked back, thinking the cop hadn't been as lucky as I had been. I saw the cop on two wheels, but actually gaining on the corner. I scrambled through the dust of the pack, trying to lose myself in the crowd. No deal; the cop had a magnet on his car. He scraped a few drivers coming through, but he got through just the same and it was just me and him again.

I feinted an outside rollaway, cutting my speed, but when he came after me, I wheeled sharp to the inside and cut close to the half-buried tires lining the pits. The cop couldn't slow enough and went into the outside retaining wall. He didn't stop though, only bounced off and kept on coming.

For another half dozen laps I kept my lead, but was concentrating so deeply that sweat cascaded down my face in rivulets. The people in the stands were jumping and screaming. This was something they'd remember. I noticed several familiar cars in the pits—they were cars I'd already lapped, some of them I'd lapped twice or more. I scoured the track itself, but there was

no one near me except the cop, and after only two more laps
we were alone on the track. The other drivers were clustered in
the pits, sitting on their cars and rooting us on. I also saw, through
the smoke and dust, the green flag signaling the approaching last
lap.

But what were laps anyway? I was just trying to stay away
from the cop. I thought of simply going out the back gate the
way I'd come in, but it was blocked with people who had poured
down from the stands for a better view. If I tried it I'd kill twenty people. Only twenty? I was considering it when I heard another
shout go up. The cop, tires nearly burning, had gotten to the
inside and had an angle on me. With only a half lap to go in
the race he drew alongside me, then blasted past. Then he turned
very slightly and let up on the gas, actually trying to force me
off the track. I saw his arms tense an instant before he hit his
brakes and spun halfway around, bringing the door on his
passenger side directly into my face—I could see the car
number—41—as clearly as if it had been painted on my eyeballs.
Our speeds were so close that, when I hit my own brakes, my
front bumper kissed his side and stuck as we both spun out of
control. When we finally stopped the cop was sitting on one side
of the finish line and I was sitting on the other; my front bumper
may have actually pushed him over. Both motors were stalled,
and for the first time I really heard the tremendous ovation that
the spectators—no longer in the stands—were whooping up.

When the cop got out of his car, the dust in the air was still
thick enough to stop spit and the smell of rubber was so strong
I might have been cooking up a pot of it on my dash. When
the cop took off his helmet, the shouting died down to a hush.
He scratched his head, took out a pad from his hip pocket, and
walked over to my car.

"Going a little fast there, weren't you?" he said.

"What is this, man? I'm supposed to be in a race here. What
did you butt in for?" I was hot under the collar, probably because
I had just run the race of a lifetime and still gotten beat. The
crowd was leaning forward to catch every word, but they didn't
really have to. The track was an echo chamber and every word

popped from my mouth like a tiny explosion.

"Speeders lose licenses," he said, and began writing out a speeding ticket. "Let me see yours, please."

"My what?"

"Your drivers license."

"I haven't got one."

"No license? What's your name?

"I don't have one of those either."

"It's a good thing I noticed you, then. Do you know what would happen if no one had a name?"

"Then anytime *one* person got a speeding ticket, we'd *all* have to pay?"

"That's right," he said solemnly. "Better follow me downtown."

Well, that was the end of my racing career. I was fined $25 for speeding and thrown in jail for contempt when I didn't say anything after the judge asked me to state my full name. I guess it doesn't pay to be a nobody.

"Nobody!" yelled Biggeorge.

"What's that?" I asked.

"Nobody's that lucky!" he screamed, tearing up his last tickets and stomping on them. I was also in a fury. I had just bet $500 on a 45-1 shot and it had come in. It paid me $22,500—the largest payoff in the history of dog racing. I now had about $120,000 that I didn't know what to do with.

"Give it to me," drooled Biggeorge as we drove back home.

"No way," I said. As I saw it, the extra $20,000 really was mine, even if the original hundred grand wasn't. And as I drove through streets even emptier and more desolate than they'd been a few hours before, I was dredging up memories of the cheers from my last race and wondering what would happen if I were to use some of the money to fix up another car. Now that I was rich I could probably hire someone to drive it for me and avoid all the hassles I'd gone through before. Or maybe I could buy a greyhound. The idea of tying Mouse Man to the rabbit's stick to train it appealed to me, and I laughed out loud.

"Funny man," said Biggeorge.

"What?"

"I mean, what's so funny, man?" he asked. "I lost money when I wanted to win and you won money when you wanted to lose."

"The season has just started, old man," I told him. "And tomorrow is another night."

Metamorphosis
of an Elvis Presley Impersonator

The bandages came off like a cocoon.

There was still some swelling and a little redness, but it faded almost as I watched. I smiled at my new reflection: now I could quit my job. Now I could hang out in better bars.

My father came to pick me up from the hospital. He looked slightly embarrassed. "No sweat, Pop," I told him. "It's cool."

A throng of middle-aged women were waiting outside the hospital. They called me the King and said they liked my moves. I dug it. I took them home with us and let them take pictures. When they began stealing my clothes I hired bodyguards to keep them out. Now they just hang around outside.

Before the operation I felt claustrophobic. Afterward, I stayed inside more and more. I enjoyed watching my room slowly take the shape of a cathedral. Each day the room grew larger by a shade. One night it split and became two rooms, then four. I hung gold discs on all the walls and bought dozens of pairs of boots. I clomped hollowly through the great halls.

Outside, newspaper reporters talk to men who are now impersonating the groupies. They get good human interest stories that double the sales of their papers. The reporters are constantly asking for, and getting, raises. The groupies make a good living selling pictures of my house. I pay them large sums of money to cut my lawn, now grown out over several acres.

My father, too, talks to the reporters. Recently he changed his name and his age. He treats me like an elder and secretly takes notes.

It seems like years ago that I lurked on the edge of things like a gargoyle. All I ever wanted was to be in the thick of it, but still I don't go out. My house has mitosed into rooms covering several large blocks. Whole families have moved in. Some of them ask me what I'm doing here. Lately, these people have threatened to evict me, so I've started buying guns. I like the feel of them, and they don't talk back to me unless I want them to. To avoid my tenants I keep strange hours and my bodyguards give me pills to help me stay awake. My doctors are worried about me and give me pills to make me sleep. I like both, but I think they're beginning to affect me in unusual ways. Once I dreamed of Quasimoto and woke in a sweat.

In the night, my house still grows outward and upward. I, too, am growing bulges where none should be. I know I should lose some weight and go on tour, but I no longer know how to get outside.

My father's room is a church tower and he has taken to giving sermons. He has purchased a keyboard synthesizer that imitates the sound of church bells. He, too, puts golden discs on the walls, and their weight is pulling plaster down in great chunks. The noise keeps me awake.

I look for my bodyguards but see only snappish eyes peering at me from the long corridors. When I look for windows I see only massive walls and falling plaster.

When my father's chimes crash from the church tower like the lost and twisted notes from someone's favorite melody, I tremble.

Abe Mott

Abe Mott lay in the Mt. Sinai Hospital in Brooklyn. He had smoked too many cigarettes in his fifty-eight years, and now he was dying. But death seemed to be scoffing at him. It had turned a strong man weak and isolated him like a bacteria in a sterile white hospital. All around him nurses whizzed past as if they were on roller skates. Doctors with spectacles and clipboards made the process of dying seem like a mere setback at a corporate sales meeting. Abe Mott knew about corporate sales meetings. For thirty years he had served as President of Mott Enterprises, which specialized in rare stones and precious gems. It was surprising to Abe Mott that his interest in such things had dwindled to nothing. He had read about the recent plunge of silver, but cared so little about it that it might have been the price of beans. There was some meaning in all this, but what?

Beside him, but behind a screen, lay an old man like himself. Abe Mott had tried to talk to the man for days now, but the only response he got was a rasping cough. Abe Mott coughed a lot too, but at least he was sociable. Perhaps he is drugged, thought Abe Mott. The coughing bothered him because it reminded him of his own dying. He was upset that he couldn't have a private room, yet whenever the coughing stopped, Abe Mott grew restless.

"Mr. Feinberg," he spoke out. "I hope you're feeling better this morning. There's something I want to discuss with you." But silence continued on the other side of the screen. Perhaps, thought Abe Mott, there is nobody on the other side of the screen at all. Maybe it was just a recording of someone coughing put there by a devil to torment him. This is what it will be like in hell, he thought, but the thought opened up new avenues of suggestion.

"Mr. Feinberg," he said, this time more loudly. "The nurse

tells me you're from the old country. Perhaps you know the little bakery down on Stekel Street in Warsaw?'' But Mr. Feinberg didn't answer. Anyway, Abe Mott did not know if Mr. Feinberg had ever lived in Warsaw. He was just trying to get him to speak. Abe Mott's grandfather—an ultraorthodox rabbi—had told him that it was bad luck to be alone with a corpse.

He tried to sit up in bed, but his strength was nearly gone. He groped for the buzzer, but couldn't find it. This is the end, he thought. Death was in the room. It had come to take away Mr. Feinberg, and why make another trip? He felt for the buzzer again but imps had hidden it from him. Imps? he thought. Devils? They were part of the old myths of his grandfather, but they were strangely disquieting nevertheless.

A small commotion outside his door made him look in that direction. A nurse bustled in and stood above him. ''Your son is here, Mr. Mott,'' she told him.

''I have no son,'' he replied.

''That's what you told us.''

''Who do you believe, then,'' he asked kindly, ''me, or my son?''

''He wants to see you,'' she said.

''Why?''

''I don't know. Maybe because he's your son.''

''Mr. Feinberg is dead,'' Abe Mott said.

''Nonsense. Mr. Feinberg is in surgery.''

''So.''

''I'm going to let your son come in for a minute or two.''

Abe Mott didn't answer. He just closed his eyes and folded his hands over his chest like a dead man. Death had not been in the room after all, but now Abe Mott wished It had. A confrontation with his son was the last thing he wanted. Better he should perish first.

Abe Mott opened his eyes only when he heard the still familiar voice of his son saying, ''Hey, Papa.''

''So,'' Abe Mott replied. ''You have come to watch me die, like a voyeur.''

''I've come to watch you get well.''

"Fat chance." Abe Mott studied his son. In the eight years since he had last seen him, Felix had grown portly. There were strands of gray hair showing through the black. A stiff smile pushed up his reddish cheeks until his eyes were nearly obscured. He was very well dressed in a tailored three-piece suit and a snappy tie. The coat was unbuttoned and Abe Mott saw a silver chain snaking into a watch pocket. Suddenly Abe Mott saw movement behind Felix: a tousled head with curious black eyes peeped out at him.

"What child is this?" asked Abe Mott in astonishment.

"My son, Papa. Your grandson."

"I didn't know I had a grandson."

"His name is David."

"Like the giant killer," said Abe Mott. The little boy looked to be seven or eight years old with curly black locks that fell over his ears. He was the handsomest little boy Abe Mott had ever seen. "Come here, David, and let me look at you."

But the boy was shy, and his father had to prompt him a bit before he stepped forward. "Hello, Grandfather," he said.

Abe Mott laughed with delight, then noticed the hopeful expression on his son's face as he watched.

"You," he said to his son. "Nothing has changed between us. I still can't bear the sight of your face. Leave me alone with the boy."

Without a word, his son started from the room. The boy followed, but his father stopped him. "Stay here with your grandfather," he said.

When Felix had gone, Abe Mott looked at the confused boy and said, "Are you frightened of your grandfather?"

"No."

"Come here, then. Bring that chair near the bed and sit by me."

"You sent Papa away," said the boy.

"Yes. But him I have known for thirty years. You I do not know at all."

"You have a bad cough. Are you dying?"

"Yes."

"I will say Kaddish for you," said the boy.

"You were brought up a Jew?" asked Abe Mott in astonishment.

"I go to Hebrew school."

"You're not a . . . a Baptist?"

"My mother is, but I like Jews better."

"What are you studying?" asked Abe Mott.

"Purim."

"Do you understand it all?"

"Most of the time I do. I ask Papa about things the rabbi says, but he can't remember. He has no time. Sometimes he paints all day long. Your father was a rabbi, wasn't he?"

Abe Mott secretly feared that the boy sitting next to him was not his grandson at all; that he was, in fact, only a spirit sent to charm him. If so, then his tongue was charmed as well, for he began to talk in the easy offhand manner that he hadn't felt since his college days. His cough stopped for the moment, driven out, perhaps, by the spirit.

"My father, no," he said. "But my grandfather was a rabbi. It was in Warsaw, which was a big city even then. There was a different sect on every block—Hasids, Zionists; there were even those who believed in false messiahs. In our house we wore skull caps and tzitzits at all times, and we had sidelocks that curled to our shoulders."

"Tell me about your grandfather," said the boy.

"My grandfather?" Abe Mott asked. It had been years, decades even, since he had talked to anyone about that stern old man.

The boy nodded shyly.

Abe Mott looked in the direction of the ceiling and remembered. "They called my grandfather Reb Barush," he told the boy. "He would seem out of place in this day and age, because he was one of those old rabbis who studied the Torah constantly and made decisions regarding the fine points of the Law. Rabbis are different now. They wear baseball caps and blue jeans. Everything is changed. My father wanted to be a rabbi too, but Reb Barush lived to be ninety, and in the area where we lived, there was a need for only one."

"Why didn't he move, then?" asked the boy.

"Families were very close in those days, David," he answered. "It was like everyone in the neighborhood was your friend, while most people who lived in other parts of the city were strangers. But my father wasn't that disappointed. He became a baker instead."

"A baker?"

"A baker," he nodded. "Bakers were very important in the old country because of all the holy days. He had to watch over each preparation of matzoh to see that it was prepared properly. The least bit of yeast, or the slightest amount of moisture before the proper time for Passover baking, and whole tubs of dough would be thrown out or given to gentiles."

Abe Mott's grandson sat at ease in the Naugahyde hospital chair. Abe Mott would have expected boys of his age to be more fidgety and less inquisitive. At least, Felix had been. Instead, the boy looked at his grandfather with a serious expression and asked, "Did he make a lot of money?"

"Oh no, at least not at first. But one day a stranger came in our shop. He wore a fur hat and satin gabardine that fell to the top of his shoes."

"I've seen men dressed like that downtown," said the boy matter-of-factly.

"This man was a little different because he was also wearing a ring that was studded with diamonds. I was only seven, but even then I helped in the shop—washing vats and sweeping the floor. My mother—may she rest in peace—called me "the ghost" because I always came home covered from head to toe in flour. We got very few rich men in our shop, so I stopped what I was doing to gape at him. This man, whose name was Chaim Mendelsson, looked at my father. "My daughter is getting married in three days," he said. "Can you provide refreshments for one hundred people?" My father's Adam's apple jumped. He had never sold more than a loaf or two of bread to any one person before. But I saw him staring at the man's expensive ring.

" 'Are there no other bakers?' he asked.

" 'They have all given me excuses.'

" 'Excuses?'

" 'One has another wedding that same day; one isn't kosher. I hired someone on Grzbalna Street, but he died.' The man looked hard into my father's face. 'Can you do the job, or not?'

" 'Of course, but . . .'

" 'But what?'

" 'It is such short notice. . . .'

"But the man handed my father a long sheet of paper and said that he would give him a bonus if he could prepare all of the baked delicacies written on it.

"So my father agreed to provide all this for the wedding. We worked night and day, checking everything off the list. My mother was angry. "Look at what happened to the other baker," she said. 'Perhaps the Heavenly One is against this wedding.' But my father paid no attention. He hired a man to work extra hours—for the Feast of the Tabernacles was approaching and we had to provide for our regular customers too."

"What kind of things did you have to make?" asked the boy excitedly.

"Ah, we baked cakes and pies and tarts and loaves of bread, finger snacks and cookies with icing. It was a happy time, let me tell you, even though we barely had time to sleep. And everything went well. It was a fine wedding; one of the biggest the town had ever seen. The next day, Chaim Mendelsson came into our shop and handed my father a set of six precious stones: a diamond, a ruby, a topaz, an amethyst, an emerald, and a small saphire. 'They are yours,' he said."

"He gave all those to him?" asked Abe Mott's grandson with wide eyes.

"Yes he did, and the first thing my father told him was that it was far too much.

" 'I am happy to see my daughter married,' said Mendelsson. And despite anything my father could say, the rich man walked out of the store. We never saw him again, but later learned that he had gone to America. My father was left staring at the brightly colored stones in his hand."

Abe Mott looked at the tousleheaded boy beside him. Caught up in the story, the boy was content now to simply listen without asking questions. And Abe Mott, too, was caught up in his reverie.

"From that point on," he continued, "our lives changed. My father didn't sell the stones as you would think, but hid them in a sock. Some nights I would see him at his desk holding one or another of the jewels up to the light. Because of the good job that we did for Chaim Mendelsson, others came to us for special occasions. But though we took in more money, we still lived the same. Father used the extra cash to buy other diamonds and rubies, which he put in the sock with the rest. Within just a few years the toe of the sock was filled with stones.

"When my grandfather, Reb Barush, heard about my father's miserliness, he chided him for it with quotations from the Mishna. He said that he paid more attention to his gems than to God.

"And maybe it was true. Gradually he began falling from the old ways. He started reading the Yiddish newspapers. Then he had other newspapers sent to him from America and studied the stock market. He still studied the Talmud and the Midrashes, but didn't spend nearly as much time on them as he used to. While he had once gone to the study house once or twice every day, he now only went on the Sabbath.

"He used to say, 'a Jew is a Jew.'

"We all knew that something was going to happen, but we were shocked when one day my father came home with steamship tickets to America for him, my mother, and me."

"What about your grandfather?" the boy asked.

"Oh, wild horses couldn't have dragged him out of Warsaw. In fact, he was furious when he heard about the tickets and sent for my father. I went too and remember my grandfather pulling his white beard—it reached almost to his waist—and pacing in his study. As soon as we closed the door, he began to shout like a lion. I don't remember much about what he said, only that he kept using a word that I suppose we would translate as iniquity. He said that there was a lot of iniquity in America.

"But my father replied that iniquity is found everywhere.

" 'You may as well step into a burning caldron!' my grand-father shouted.

" 'There is opportunity in America,' my father said. 'It is hard to do anything in Poland when you are always hungry and the gentiles treat you like cow dung.'

" 'You are better off than most gentiles.'

" 'And for how long? I'm going to take the chance while I have it.'

" 'The end of the world must be near!' Reb Barush cried, but my father didn't think so. Mother wept and wailed, sure that we would all die on the ship, or worse, that we would fall into gentile ways once we got to New York.

"But that isn't what happened. In fact, my father remained a devout Jew and contributed a lot of money to Jewish causes. He still loved gems though, and after a few years of baking mat-zoht in America, he became a dealer of jewels. When I graduated from college, I helped him."

Abe Mott stopped speaking and looked at his small listener. David was about the same age as *he* had been when Chaim Mendelsson had strutted like a chicken into his father's bakery. The boy—Abe Mott's grandson—had certainly gotten over his initial fright quickly. He looked at Abe Mott eagerly.

"I bore you with such old stories, don't I?" asked Abe Mott.

"I'm not bored," the boy replied.

Abe Mott reached out to fluff the boy's hair and was surprised to find that he barely had the strength to raise his arm. God should not allow his creatures to die weak, he thought. His own father had died in the prime of life, knocked to the earth by a car at rush hour. Abe Mott had to take over the entire business then. As he reflected on those years, Abe Mott knew that he had done well. Soon after his twenty-fifth birthday he married a fine woman. A year later she gave him a handsome son. But then something had gone wrong. His beautiful wife died in childbith, along with his next child. His son refused to go to Hebrew school. He ran away from home when he was fifteen, stole from a grocery store and was arrested. The shame and disgrace nearly killed Abe Mott. He managed to get his son freed without a sentence, but at home

Felix withdrew into himself. He began writing vicious sketches of the neighbors, and drew caricatures in pen and ink. Even then, Abe Mott realized that the sketches were good, but he was appalled.

"I have not brought you up to be a bohemian," he told Felix.

"What, then," Felix answered. "A rabbi?"

"You are acting in ways I can't understand."

"So don't try, then."

"Is this how you talk to your father?"

"Maybe if you had talked to *me* more it would be different."

It was true. Since the death of his wife, Abe Mott had been a taciturn man. Perhaps he had even become a little mad. He wanted vague things for Felix. Happiness and success were part of it, of course, but somehow, Abe Mott felt duty bound to provide these things for Felix himself. Yet he avoided voicing his views. Instead, he sent his son to finishing school, then to college, but Felix secretly dropped out of business school and began taking art classes. He got a job in a bookstore and moved out of the house. Then he met a young woman from Alabama and married her without a word to Abe Mott. It was too much. When Felix brought his new bride to meet him, Abe Mott screamed at his son and ordered him out of his house.

Abe Mott longed for a cigarette, but he knew that he had smoked his last months before. Even then he had almost coughed his lungs out and suffocated.

Lying in a hospital bed put a new perspective on things. His actions of eight years before now reminded him of the rantings of his grandfather, who had never forgiven his son for going to America. Had Abe Mott been equally unforgiving and hard-hearted? His son had become a political cartoonist, then a well-known painter. He had read about him in the newspapers, had even seen a reproduction of one of his paintings—a study of Hasidic Jews in New York's Hell's Kitchen. And now he was raising his own son as a Jew.

Abe Mott was shocked as he remembered that he himself had not been to the synagogue for years. He had chain-smoked cigars and cigarettes even on the Sabbath. What has happened to me?

thought Abe Mott. And what does it all mean?

His grandson was still looking at him patiently. "You're tired," the boy said.

"No," said Abe Mott, but even his voice had become weak. Something important was going through Abe Mott's head, but very languidly, as if his thoughts had been slowed to a trickle by his weakness.

"Grandfather," began the boy, "I'm sorry my mother is a Baptist. . . ."

"We are all what we must be," Abe Mott answered, but this sounded like a lie. For his son it was true, for he had been driven to become a painter. And his father was driven to come to America by the glinting light of six jewels. But was he—Abe Mott—the man he had to be? He fumbled for the buzzer and found it. But the strength this took caused him to gasp and nearly fall out of bed.

When the nurse rushed in, he realized that he was still pressing the buzzer. He began a coughing spasm that seemed endless.

"Shame on you, young man," the nurse admonished the boy. "You have upset your grandfather. Shoo now."

Abe Mott tried to sit up. "No," he gasped. "The boy has reminded me of God."

"You've had far too much excitement for one day," she said.

"And far too little for a lifetime," he replied. He felt some of his strength returning. Suddenly a stretcher was wheeled in. Was it for him? No, it was Mr. Feinberg back from surgery. He was awake and looked kindly at Abe Mott. He even seemed to shrug, as if to say that he had tasted death and had found it to be only so so.

Abe Mott was happy to see Mr. Feinberg, even though he had forgotten the things he wanted to discuss with him. As Mr. Feinberg was returned to his bed behind the screen, Abe Mott noticed the old man's gleaming wedding ring—a diamond circled by a cluster of small rubies. He admired the polish and the setting. Hoping that his own father would intercede for him in heaven, Abe Mott said, "Send my son in now."

Souls

Zimmer limps into the alley looking like a clown chasing shadows. One of his shoes has come loose, falling away into the black alley like something dropped through a hole. His shirttail is a furled white flag and cold sweat drenches his face. His hot breath precedes him across the pavement in the forty-degree night, choked from his throat in spasmodic bursts. In his haste he kicks an empty oil can, sending it clattering across the asphalt and into a factory wall. The alleyway is a narrow, endless well and Zimmer, though he hurries on, cannot see the man he is pursuing.

He stops; just ahead he hears the sound of scattering tin, another slapping of running footsteps. In front of him, the faint shadow of another man tries to flatten itself against a wall. But the shadows are not deep enough to hide the heaving body, nor dense enough to blacken the breath.

Zimmer trembles forward. He hears the chattering of teeth, but does not know if the sound is coming from himself or his quarry. When he is close enough to see the terrified pleas of the huddling man's eyes, he closes his own and shoots six bullets into the man's body. He vomits white air as he runs from the alley, clutching the gun like another hand.

He runs until his swollen muscles give out, then grabs onto a fluted lamppost like a drunk. He is a murderer now. The thought makes him so queasy that he almost loses his grip on the lamppost. A murderer! His life is ruined, but what else could he have done? Smiled and done a Henny Youngman impersonation? (Say, I must be in the wrong house; *nobody* would get in bed with *my* wife!) A man has to have self-respect. Zimmer straightens up and smooths his coat. He notices that he is now in a residential section of town—one near his own home. He has run farther than he thought. He raises a hand to his head, but instead of combing the ruffled hair, he tears it violently.

"Zim." The familiar voice stops him, freezes a smile on his face. It is the voice of the man he has just killed. He darts terrified glances into nearby yards and shrubs. All the houses along the block are dark. The streets carry only the shadows of parked cars. Many blocks back, a yellow light turns red, but no cars are stopped or released by its changing.

"And what was it that I done that made you to go and do this terrible thing to me?"

Theo is dead; the block is empty, yet the voice Zimmer hears is Theo's. He hears it as clear as if it were injected directly into his brain.

"Zim?"

"What?" Zimmer whispers, but the word is less a response to the voice than a question to the universe. Theo is unquestionably dead. Then how does he come to be talking?

"Who would have ever thought that you'd go around playing God?"

The voice is so penetrating that, for an instant, Zimmer thinks he is in contact with the supernatural. He trembles—the first person since Moses to speak to God. I have forgotten the consequences, he thinks, of rash acts. "But, God," he asks aloud, "Is what I did so bad that you have to punish me personally? You couldn't have sent down a flunky? I mean, what would *you* do if you found some dummy conjugating in your conjugal bed? Not that you'd ever do that kind of thing, of course."

"Even to God you'd be a comedian, wouldn't you Zim?"

Why, thinks Zimmer, does God have Theo's voice?

"There's no God, Zim."

This is too much. "What do you want and how do I make you go away?" Zimmers asks in a whisper.

"You should have asked me that before you shot me."

"You're dead, so how can you be talking to me? You're making me look suspicious to all these people looking out their curtains. I don't feel well. I want to go home."

"Don't start cracking up, Zim. I need you."

"Like you needed my wife?"

"Much more."

So this is what madness is, Zimmer thinks. He uses the window of a parked car for a mirror. Face white, clothes like balloons, electric hair. Ready for the looney bin, anyone can see it. Zimmer recollects, like a reflection, the image of a man he had seen years before. It was in a park in Hoboken. Two puppies were chasing each other in the grass. A tramp with a stubble of white beard was talking to a crowd about transmigration of souls. Spit flew from his mouth like machine gun bullets.

Soon, thinks Zimmer, I too will be drooling.

"What did the man say, Zim?" asks the voice.

"What man?" Zimmer asks, no longer bothering to whisper or to look around for the voice.

"The old bum with his overcoat so stained with wine and dirty from sleeping in the grass."

"There was no man. I've never been to Hoboken."

This realization comes as a surprise. Zimmer has certainly never been to Hoboken, yet he remembers seeing the old man there as plain as he remembers anything. "A man's soul is like a breath," the old man had shouted to the crowd. "When you die, your soul is expelled from your body and is like a tramp that roams where it will. All of you think that God chooses the direction your soul goes, but that ain't the way it happens. It's all circumstances, har har."

Zimmer chortles. Circumstances. It was circumstances that made me shoot Theo. Circumstances that will probably get me the electric chair.

"No way." That voice again. "Mitigating circumstances. No jury will convict a man for what you did, Zim."

Zimmer pays no attention to the voice. He is thinking about the tramp in Hoboken. A cop had run him off with a stick. He remembers that the man had once committed a crime. He had choked his nagging wife and gone to jail for many years. People said he went crazy there.

But he hadn't been crazy at all; Zimmer knows that now. His dead wife's soul had inhabited his body as recompense.

"It's a just reward, ain't it, Zim?"

"What?"

"To have to carry my soul around with you from now on."

"I don't know what you mean."

"You'll have my thoughts as well as your own. Even when you're asleep you'll be dreaming about things I would dream about, as well as your own dreams."

"Do you expect me to believe that?"

"*I* grew up in Hoboken, Zim."

Zimmer is struck speechless. So it's all true.

"Take a life and gain a soul. Now you have two. There are stranger things."

"I'd rather be dead."

"You don't mean that, Zim!"

"Oh yes, yes I do!"

"We'll make a nice pair, Zim. We'll be friends. It could be worse. You could be that old man. His wife shared his soul after he killed her. He should've been so lucky to have a soul like me. It's a wonder he didn't hang himself."

"He should've."

"See there, we agree on something already."

"I'm a murderer. I feel terrible. My wife is unfaithful and won't even care about what I've done. Now I've got my worst enemy as a critic for the rest of my life."

"Well, look at the bright side. Let's face it, Zim, all comedians secretly want to kill their agents. You've done something nobody else has, and it'll go over big. Look at Richard Pryor. He goes berserk and shoots holes through his wife's Cadillac. The judge lets him off and he writes it into his material. His career starts to take off. Then he sets himself on fire and makes jokes about *that*. Now he needs a rake to gather up all his bucks. Think of how well a murder will go over."

"I'd rather be electrocuted."

"That's out. We'll cop a temporary insanity plea."

"I don't think it's temporary. I should have saved myself pain and shot myself instead of you."

"Maybe so."

"I'm tired. What made you go after Jenny, anyway?"

"What makes mountain climbers climb?"

"I never thought of Jenny as Mount Everest."

"More like the Matterhorn."

"What's the difference?"

"Attainability. The Matterhorn used to be unclimbable when it was young and untried. Now, everybody climbs up there."

"I don't want to hear any more of your jokes."

"I thought that was pretty good."

"It was stupid and in bad taste. Look, I don't need any failed funnyman telling me stale jokes."

"How do you know I . . ."

"How do I know you wanted to be a comedian like Rodney Dangerfield? How do I know that the first time you stood in front of an audience made up of two-bit weirdos and drunks that you froze up like a statue? Well, you got laughed at all right, and I know it because this souls shtick is a two-way street."

"All right. You've made your point. Watch that manhole; some kids have taken the cover off."

"I can see without your help."

"All right. Okay."

Zimmer turns the corner into his own block. "Do a lot of guys screw Jenny?" he asks.

"One less than before, but she won't want that much because of my demise."

"Maybe I'll have to kill her, too." Zimmer shudders.

"And be stuck with another soul? Don't be a glutton for punishment. Jenny's a bitch. The sooner you're rid of her the better. She only married you for your money anyway."

"What do you know about it?"

"Everything, and I'm telling you for your own good. Chalk Jenny up to experience. Get rid of her and marry a nice Jewish girl like your old mother dreamed."

"I don't like Jewish women. I didn't even like my mother."

"So better yet, be a bachelor again like I was. That was the life, boy. Listen, Zim, a lot of women come through my office. They're looking for a break and don't care what they have to do to get it. I'll clue you in on who can be made and who can't so you won't have to waste any time."

"I don't want other women, and I won't have someone I've just killed telling me how to live."

"We're a single person now, Zim. Try and realize this. You have to listen to what I say."

"I won't have it!"

"Calm down. Look at your clothes, they're a mess. And what's happened to your other shoe? You can't let the neighbors see you like this. They'll think you're drunk. And Jenny. Don't tell her you caught up with me. Who knows what she might do."

"I don't think I'm going to be able to handle this."

"Look, Zim, you just shot a guy. Naturally you're tense, upset. Go in the house and take a bicarbonate. I've already forgiven you. Confide in me. Open up a little. I can help."

"Why don't you shut up?"

"We're home now. Don't be wild. Comb your hair and put that gun away."

Zimmer walks up the driveway of his home. He is dizzy and nearly stumbles. The gun he used many streets back has never left his grip, and his muscles are frozen around it from constantly squeezing the handle. He looks like a man who is plagued with bees flying around his head.

The door is unlocked. Zimmer opens it and walks into a brightly lit parlor with a huge sofa and matching armchairs. Two low tables are spread out with theater magazines arranged in neat fans. A series of paintings of the New York skyline dash the walls.

"Jenny!" he shouts, but Theo's voice cuts him off.

"Be quiet, Zim. It's late. People are sleeping. Is it the cops you want?"

"Jenny! Where are you, goddam it?" He searches the house. Each room has every light burning, but each is immaculately, silently empty. In his wife's bedroom Zimmer notices that her cosmetic case is gone; the vanity table has been swept clean to the doily. The wardrobe is empty. He runs back out into the parlor, almost tripping over a table, and begins beating himself on the head with the pistol barrel.

"Hey, Zim, cut that out. That hurts! Let her go. We'll be happy just the two of us."

Zimmer rushes into his own bedroom. He snatches some bullets from a drawer and hastily reloads the gun. His right hand is cramped around the handle and he has to open the breech and load the bullets with his left. Several fall to the floor and scatter.

"What we need is a little sleep. Let's think about all this tomorrow. She probably just went out by herself to think things over. She'll be back. Everything will be hunky dory again."

"Don't humor me!" Zimmer shouts. "I'm the funnyman, remember?" He begins poking into closets, as if looking for a hidden man. Then he spots a note on the bed.

> You probably killed Theo. If I had known you had it in you to do that, I might not have hated you so much all these years. My lawyer will contact you tomorrow about our divorce. Contest it and I'll go to Reno and get one anyway and then testify against you for murder. You'll notice that I've withdrawn most of our savings. Use the rest to buy yourself a comic book.
>
> J

"I told you she was a bitch. Never trust women, Zim. They're all alike. They'll take everything you got and then want your nuts too."

Zimmer sits down and combs his sparse hair with his hand.

"But it's nothing to worry about; there's plenty of laughs in a lifetime. And think of the money you'll save by being your own agent."

Zimmer gets up and slowly walks through the house turning out the lights.

"Time to sleep, hey, Zim?"

"Yes."

"Thataboy."

When the house is as black as the alley had been, Zimmer sits down on the sofa and stares toward the curtains.

"What's this?" Theo's voice asks.

Zimmer remains silent.

"This is unhealthy, Zim. You're not thinking of nothing.

Nobody thinks of just nothing. What do you want to ostracize me for? Let me tell you this joke.''

"No," Zimmer interrupts. He hears his voice echo as if through an empty auditorium. "Let me tell you one."

"Now you're talking."

"There was this guy, see?" His voice is soft, almost tender. The pistol is solid in his hand.

"Yeah? Go on."

"That's it," Zimmer says. "That's the joke. There is no more."

Action

An attractive woman of thirty three sat behind a small desk in a very large building. She was a newspaper reporter and, although she was alone in her office, she was only pretending to be absorbed in the story she was typing. Several finished pages of yellow copy lay in a neat pile on the desk while others had been crumpled and tossed towards the wastebasket. When the door opened, she barely glanced up, although her heart quickened perceptibly.

"Hi," she said, making it sound as offhand as she could.

The newcomer took off his hat and put it on a hatstand near the door. He then made a point of loosening his tie. "Hot in here," he mumbled.

"You look as cool as a cucumber to me—as always." The woman had the faintest trace of a smile.

"Hmph!" exclaimed the man, who was taller than the average, and very conservatively dressed. He took off his coat and hung it over the back of a chair. He then took a handkerchief out of his shirt pocket and passed it over his forehead. A dark sweat stain was obvious under his raised arm. The woman at the typewriter swore under her breath. Now it was the man's turn to smile faintly.

"Did you finish your part of the story?" she asked.

"I'm going to finish it up right now." The man started to sit down at his desk but, seeing he was out of typing paper, changed his mind and walked across the room to the supply cabinet. Suddenly a shot rang out, bringing a smell of acrid smoke and a triumphant cry. The man dived to the floor and lay there cowering.

"Stop trembling, Clark, or should I say, Superman?"

"What are you talking about, Lois, and what are you doing with that gun?"

"Don't play games, Clark. I've given ten years of my life to prove that you and Superman are the same person. I've finally succeeded."

Clark Kent got up from the office floor and brushed himself off. "Lois," he said seriously, "You have to get this silly notion out of your head."

"Clark, I just shot you with a 38-caliber Smith and Wesson at a range that even a blind person couldn't have missed at. Yet the bullet bounced right off you."

"What bullet, Lois?"

"What do you mean?" Lois asked, a bit confused.

"If it bounced off me, where is it now?"

"How should I know?"

"And where did it hit me?"

"There, in the small of your back."

"And you couldn't have missed?"

"Not a chance, Clark."

"Because I'm *not* Superman, I would be either dead or paralyzed if you had really hit me. But even if I *am* Superman, there would be a hole in my shirt. Do you see one?" He turned around for her to inspect his shirt from the back.

"I don't understand this."

"Luckily, this is another of your little jokes. You probably loaded that pistol with blanks and shot into the air just to see me dive for cover. And who wouldn't have? But why are you always trying to make me look like a fool? After all, I have feelings too."

"But the bullets are real. Here, take a look."

"This is going too far, Lois. What if you had miscalculated and shot the wrong one? You would be all over the front page of tonight's final—and with someone else's byline."

"They were *all* real."

"Sure, Lois."

"I know what you're going to say now, Clark. If they were all real, where is the slug?"

"Even if you did miss me, you would have hit the filing cabinet."

"It hit your shirt and bounced onto a soft place—your coat maybe. You treated your shirt with some chemical that makes bullets impenetrable."

"Give me your scissors, Lois." Clark Kent took the scissors and, holding his shirt away from his skin, jabbed several holes through the material.

Lois looked puzzled, then spoke up. "Oh no, Clark. Let *me* do that." She jabbed another hole, this time in the back of the shirt, and her face fell.

"Are you satisfied now, Lois?" He looked exasperated.

"You've beaten me again, Clark."

"You've just succeeded in making me look foolish again."

"I'm the fool, Clark, for not stabbing you with the scissors when I had the chance, but I have one last question."

"What's that, Lois?"

"Why are you so anxious to prove to me that you're *not* Superman?"

"You kill me, Lois."

Just then the office door flew open and the two reporters looked around to see an older man with a red face and a shock of white hair. He was coatless, and his tie was loosened inches down his neck. "What was that noise? I thought I heard a gunshot!"

"I'm covering the Special Olympics tomorrow, Chief, and I borrowed a starter's gun from one of the organizers. Clark shot it off accidentally. You know how clumsy he is."

"Yes, I do, and sometimes you worry me, Kent. You're getting as bad as Olsen. And don't call me Chief."

"Sorry, Chief, I mean Mr. White."

"That's better. Now as long as you made me run down here by firing that blasted pistol, how's the rest of that story coming?"

"Just finishing up."

"By the way—you both did a fine job in helping to expose that ring of dope peddlers, but if it hadn't been for Superman, you'd probably be in the obituary column today. And you, Kent, where were you when all the shooting started?"

"Well, that's kind of delicate."

"Delicate my foot. You were probably hiding somewhere."

"Don't be hard on him, Ch—Mr. White. You know how Clark has been complaining of stomach pains for the last couple of days. It just happened that he had to rush to the bathroom right when the crooks drove up."

"Never mind, then. I suppose I should compliment you personally, Kent, for the digging you did in finding out about that drug ring in the first place."

"That's part of my job," answered Clark, but his face glowed with pleasure.

"But it wasn't part of your job to get yourselves killed. Here's an easy assignment. I want both of you to go out tonight and get drunk. Have a big meal and enjoy yourselves. Put it on your expense account."

"Why, Chief!" exclaimed Lois happily.

"What did someone say about gold lurking in the most unlikely places?" laughed Clark. "Of course it's taken years . . ."

"Just get out of here!" roared Perry White. "And don't call me Chief!"

*   *   *   *   *

"I know Clark is really Superman," mused Lois Lane, "but how can I prove it?" It was later in the afternoon and she was taking a shower, letting the warm water drench her hair and run in streams down her back.

"Maybe he can read minds," she thought to herself. This was something new—what if he *could* read minds. That would explain how Clark kept her virtually at bay. He could prepare for an emergency before it happened. Maybe if she tried to keep her mind on something else.

She soaped her breasts, letting the thick lather build up like cream on her skin—her thirty-three-year-old skin. Her youth was gone, and for what? For the pleasure of shooting a pistol at Clark Kent? And if she tried to stab him tonight with a steak knife would she just happen to pick the spot where Clark kept his cigarette case (Clark didn't smoke, but he would find a way to explain its presence nevertheless), or would he, for some reason known only to a secret few, be wearing a bullet-proof vest? Old habits die hard. She had been working on this Superman thing for years now, but she was at her wit's end. The sudden thought came to her that perhaps Superman was God. The thought made her feel exposed a little and afraid.

*   *   *   *   *

Clark Kent sat in his room with his legs propped up on his dining table. The few dirty dishes, as well as a half-empty fruit bowl, were only for show—eating gave him indigestion by making his usually dormant digestive system begin working. His stomach was rumbling with the mere anticipation of his meal with Lois Lane later in the evening. And his mind was working as well.

"That fool Lois," he thought. "She's going to expose me someday at just the wrong time. Just at the moment the president is being assassinated, or at the same instant someone is pushing a nuclear button. Maybe I should move away from Metropolis." It was better not to think about it. His thoughts flashed instead to the scene of that morning. He had to give Lois a lot of credit. She tried hard, but after ten years or so of studying her habits he found he could often anticipate her routines. He watched her carefully now.

From the moment he had walked in the Daily Planet Building that morning, he had been watching her with his X-ray vision. She was very cunning. She never once looked up from her typing. And it had been her story she was typing, not some fake set of words for the sake of appearances. Could it be that she wouldn't try anything today? It was too much to hope for, especially after he had made her swallow that line about an upset stomach and a trip to the bathroom. To be on the safe side he stopped at a water fountain and used it to give his shirt an underarm stain. That was a nice touch. That and the beads of sweat on his forehead. Outside the door he had quickly scanned her desk. Nothing suspicious but a lead box. But a lead box was *very* suspicious. Here, Lois had gone overboard. After all, what could she possibly be using a lead box for except to hide something from Superman? Quickly he had turned his watch crystal toward his arm. The back was a very effective mirror he had designed for just such occasions. As he went to the cabinet to get typing paper he was watching Lois take the gun out of its shielding and fire it. It had been an easy matter to flick out a hand at super speed and catch the bullet before he dove to the floor in mock terror.

What was the matter with her anyway? Why this mania? He was always uneasy around Lois Lane, as if she could see through his clothing, instead of vice versa.

*   *   *   *   *

"You live dangerously, Clark."

"Why do you say that, Lois?"

"I didn't know we were coming to Chinatown."

"We can go somewhere else."

"Oh no. I wouldn't miss this for anything. I just thought, well, you know."

"Know what, Lois?"

"Well, you're usually such a coward. I wouldn't have dreamed you would decide to come here of all places."

"Maybe I'm trying to prove something to myself."

"And to me, too, Clark?" she asked mischievously.

"Whatever do you mean by that, Lois?"

"Nothing, Clark. I'm just worried about the gang wars, that's all. It's silly exposing yourself to danger just to prove a point."

"They *have* been in the news a lot lately."

"Oh well, maybe we'll get a story while we're here."

"I'm game if you are, Lois."

A waiter approached with a bow and said, "Come with me, please." He led the couple to a table against the wall, about midway between the door and the kitchen. Lois looked around in awe. All around them were pictures of the animals that represented the Chinese years—huge murals of rice paper flowing across the walls. They ranged from the fantastic to the grotesque. They sat between a giant fire-breathing horse, rearing and pawing the sky in anger and fear, and a snake—mouth wide open and ready to receive its superlong tail. Even in the subdued light the colors were vivid.

"Golly," she breathed.

"You've never been here before, Lois?"

"Only on assignment, and I never really noticed anything but bodies and police."

"A reporter spends too much time on grim details. We need to look around us and study what life really is."

"Why Clark, what a perceptive and intelligent thing to say."

"You don't know me at all, Lois."

"I guess I don't."

"You've been so busy trying to prove I'm Superman that you haven't given any thought to me as a person."

"I don't know what to say, Clark. You're right and I apologize. Maybe I can start making it up to you. But what's this?"

"Mao-tai, Lois. Have a glass."

"Mmm. It's good."

"Do you think I'm a good reporter, Lois?"

"A good reporter? I suppose so. Why?"

"You've never really thought about it, have you?"

"I . . . I guess not."

"But think back on all the things I've written, all the stories I've broken. Think of the leads I've given *you*, Lois."

"I guess I just always thought Superman got you those leads. After all, if you were Superman it would be easy for you to . . ."

"Stop it, Lois!"

"Forgive me, Clark."

"And what kind of *writer* am I, even if you forget the investigative work I've done?"

"You're a *good* writer, Clark."

"You're just trying to make me feel good. The fact is, you've probably never even given a thought to my writing. Nor to what kind of person I am."

"I admit it, Clark, but as of tonight I'm turning over a new leaf."

"Fine, Lois. Have another glass of Mao-tai."

"Thank you."

"Do you drink often, Lois?"

"No I don't. Why do you ask?"

"It's just that you seem a little high already, but maybe you're just more lively than I ever realized."

"More *fun*?"

"Well, yes. More fun."

"You would have known that all along if you had bothered to ask me out once in a while."

"Yes . . . I suppose."

"Don't hem and haw, Clark. Why haven't you ever asked me out? Don't you find me attractive?"

"Very much so."

"Then why?"

"It's none of my business, Lois, but I've never seen you on a date before. I thought . . ."

"Thought what, Clark?"

"Well, that you didn't go out with men."

"Why Clark, I'm shocked! You thought I was gay?"

"What else was there to think?"

"How idiotic! Just because you never saw me on a date. For that matter, I've never seen *you* on one either. So how can that logically follow . . .? Oh no, Clark. Are *you* gay?"

"Certainly not, Lois."

"Whew! I was just getting to like you."

"To like me?"

"It's like I'm a different person here, Clark. And with new and exotic surroundings, good food, and a bottle of wine, you seem like a new person too."

"I'm glad."

"I never realized how handsome you are. And well built, too. You should show off your body more, Clark. Those clothes don't do you justice."

"I don't know . . ."

"Really, Clark. You're a handsome guy."

Clark Kent had been so charmed by Lois Lane's flattery that he had not noticed that it had started to rain. He had not seen the black sedan swish through the puddles near the curb and stop in front of the restaurant, nor had he seen the two men step out clutching tommy guns to their sides. The heavy footsteps of wet boots, loud by Superman's standards, were lost on the unsuspecting pair of reporters until the men—one bulky and hairy with very thick spectacles, the other skinny and mustachioed—burst through the door and screamed, "Freeze!"

Lois dropped her chopsticks in mid-sentence and whispered, "Clark, do something!"

"How can I, Lois?"

"What do they want?"

"They seem to be looking for someone."

In fact, the two men had separated—the thin one remaining by the door while his rough-looking companion scowled at the diners at each table as he slowly made his way across the room. "Don't none of youse move," growled the man by the door.

"Is it another gang war?" Lois asked, trembling.

"I don't think so, Lois. These fellows aren't Chinese. They're just hoods."

"Who're ya calling hoods, mister?" shouted the burly man. As he approached the table he began squinting at Clark and Lois and his eyes lit up in a bitter smile. "Well, well, who do we have here? Kent and Lane—two *Planet* reporters. Just the people we're looking for."

"You're l-looking for us?" stammered Lois.

"That's right, lady. You thought you were real smart rounding up our pals in that drug bust, didn't you? But you won't live to testify."

"But we don't have to testify," Clark put in quickly. "The police have more than enough evidence without us."

"Oh yeah?"

"Yes, that's right." Lois answered.

"Well, I'm gonna shoot ya anyway."

"Why?" cried Lois.

"Do ya think we're gonna let ya get away with it? Because of you, our pals are in the slammer. And anyway, how do ya think it would look t'our pals if we busted in here and *didn't* kill ya?"

"Maybe we can work something out," said Clark.

"Oh yeah?" The big man squinted at him. From across the

room his partner yelled out, "Shoot 'em, Jack!"

"You can't even see us," remarked Clark. "How can you shoot us?"

"This is for being a wise guy," said the man. He leveled his tommy gun at Clark Kent and fired off a burst of shells. Strangely, Clark remained sitting and smiling while Lois Lane slumped forward in a swoon.

"You missed me," said Clark Kent. "Now give me that gun." As he spoke he stood up and wrestled the gun from the smaller but bulkier man.

"Stop right there!" shrilled the skinny man, looking frantic from his post at the restaurant door. "Drop that gun or I'll level everybody in the place!"

"Everybody's already on the floor," said Clark.

"You're not, though, and I'm a dead shot at this range."

Clark was having fun. With Lois having fainted, he could use any super power he wished, as long as he made no one else in the restaurant suspicious. The burly hood, Jack, was so obviously blind that it would take no special effort to convince anyone that he had simply missed, yet Clark had made sure that none of the bullets had gone astray to hurt someone else. He had deflected each bullet with a short puff of super breath, guiding them harmlessly into a wall behind him. It had taken little strength to wrest away the man's gun—after all, Lois had said he was a fine specimen of a man, even as Clark Kent. Now, everyone in the restaurant had dived to the floor and were mostly out of sight under the tables. Clark smiled at the gunman at the door, who was looking around him wildly and sweating. "Your pants are on fire," he said.

"Don't g-give me any of . . . Yeow!" He dropped his gun and began tugging off his trousers in a frenzy. By this time his partner had made his way to the door, stumbling over several tables as he bulled his way forward. Thoroughly frightened, the two men made a mad dash to their car, still parked on the curb. Clark laughed to see the skinny one running with only a shirt and shoes, his bare flesh red and stubbly like a plucked chicken. Jack quickly fell down in the mud near the curb and came up in blackface. But their surprises were not over yet, for when they reached their car, they saw that it was in the process of being stolen by a gang of Chinese thugs. "You get in," smiled one of the Chinese. "You drive us. Then mebby we not cut you up so bad, yes?"

As the car drove off, haltingly, the diners began to get up from the floor and brush themselves off. The waiters and cooks looked out from the kitchen. Even Lois Lane stirred from her plate of rice.

"What happened, Clark?" she asked dazedly. "What are you doing with that gun?"

"I took it away from the thug."

"You're usually so timid though. What made you so macho? You didn't even flinch when that man pointed his gun at you."

"Maybe it was the things you said about me, Lois."

"But what happened?"

"They just panicked and started firing wildly. Luckily, no one was hurt. Some passersby caught them outside and made citzens' arrests."

"And I missed the whole thing! I fainted like I had never seen a gun before."

"Maybe it was the wine."

"Could be."

Several diners stopped by the table to clap Clark Kent on the back and say how brave he was to take the gun away from the myopic hoodlum. "You save us all," they said.

Lois stared at Clark in fascination and admiration. When the last diner had gone, and she had drunk another half bottle of Mao-tai while they gave their story to the police (and by phone to the *Daily Planet* office), she asked him timidly, "Will you show me where you live, Clark?"

"Very well, Lois."

*   *   *   *   *

"You're wonderful, Clark," Lois breathed.

Clark didn't reply. He was thinking about his increasingly hazardous existence around Lois Lane. He knew that Lois had been puzzled and even irritated at her weakness in the restaurant.

Whether or not she had hired the two thugs to follow them to the restaurant and scare him into revealing his identity as Superman was something he may never know. Yet it was a possibility he could not dismiss. It had been in his mind as soon as the two appeared in the doorway. He had been gradually, by using super inhalation, removing much of the oxygen, and indeed, much of the air itself, from Lois's breathing space. This asphyxiated her temporarily, while making it seem like she had fainted. He had then been able to do as he wished, but what would Lois do next? Already he had to beg an excuse to go to the bathroom so Lois's probing fingers would be able to touch bare skin rather than a Superman suit.

"You have a great body," she hissed. "Do you sleep with many women?"

Once again, Clark didn't answer, but this time he was intent on his own movements. He had watched others doing it often enough, but actually getting into it was tricky. Touching Lois's warm flesh brought out new sensations in him.

Lois was squirming. "Oh," she breathed. "Oh. Let me on top for a while. You're a strong silent type after all, aren't you, Clark? You don't know how you're making me feel. I'm, oh God, Clark, I'm coming!"

Clark was also happy. He had pleased her and had convinced her at last that he was Clark Kent, and more important, that Clark Kent was a man worthy of love and respect. As Lois continued moaning her excitement to all corners of the room, Clark wished he had tried this long ago, not only on Lois, but on Lana Lang before her. He remembered using his X-ray vision to watch her undress. In fact, he had watched her do a great number of things.

Suddenly he began to feel wonderful. Everything tingled and sparks flew in his head. He nearly thrashed off the bed.

The force of Clark's orgasm sent Lois shooting upwards and out against the wall. Her head hit the baseboard and she saw stars. Tingling in every possible area of her body, she rubbed her head and looked at Clark's writhing body with awe.

"Golly, Superman," she smiled.

In Canton

When Xin Jingyu arrived home carrying her new baby daughter, she did not see her mother-in-law crouched behind the bamboo chair. She saw only the switches, sticking out from the back of the chair like a bizarre floral arrangement. She knew that backs of chairs are not decorated with sticks, but before she could investigate, the old woman jumped up and, with a cry that would have given an emperor fright, raised the switches over her head and began beating Jingyu across the neck and shoulders with them.

Although Jingyu was startled, it wasn't a complete surprise that Liu Shang should behave like a lunatic. In fact, she had been trying hard not to expect such behavior. The old woman's face was livid with a combination of ferocity and sadness. The hundreds of lines on her face looked like ancient calligraphy. Jingyu carefully set her infant down on the floor, shielding the baby from Shang's wrath, and turned back to the old woman, who was now chanting some nonsense in the Hakka dialect. The younger woman snatched the switches from the older one's hand.

"Stop that, you old bitch," she said. "This is 1982." She snapped the twigs into small pieces and dropped them in the old woman's hair.

"May your brain be removed and your skull filled with hedgehogs," the old woman cried, "for treating your husband's old mother so!"

"My husband's old mother should mind her own business."

"Ha!" shouted the old woman, her facial lines forming and reforming the Chinese characters on her cheeks. "Someday *you* will be someone's old mother. What then, uppity one? Where is a son to take care of you?"

"I can take care of myself," replied Jingyu.

"May your teeth rot from your mouth before you are thirty."

Shang was talking softer now, almost mumbling as she bent down and busied herself with picking up the pieces of twigs and placing them in a ratty wicker basket.

"I go to the dentist all the time," Jingyu replied, lifting up her young daughter from the floor.

"Humph. A dentist from Canton; what good can she be?" Shang was now picking pieces of the twigs from her hair.

"Maybe she could wire your jaws shut," Jingyu said.

* * * * *

Jingyu sat in the mess hall holding little Peng in her lap and talking to her friend Cao Lin. Lin was one of the commune's two dentists. A short, pudgy woman with short hair and wire-rimmed spectacles, Lin had been sent by the People to work in this out-of-the-way village commune as penance for some secret anti-Party indiscretion. She was in her early thirties while Jingyu was only twenty, but Jingyu liked talking to her because she was one of the only people in the seven villages who spoke fluently both in Cantonese and Mandarin—Jingyu's native dialect. She also loved hearing about Canton—that mysterious megapolis at the end of the river.

"In Canton they are wearing Western blouses," Cao Lin was saying.

"What colors?" Jingyu asked excitedly.

"All colors."

Jingyu looked at her own green Yenan jacket and trousers. "Everything is so different there," she sighed. "The only thing grand about this village is the mess hall." In fact, the mess hall was a converted temple, with long ornamental tables and carvings in teak and brick. Even after living in the village all her life she still loved the richly colored stained glass windows and the murals that covered many of the walls. She enjoyed walking in the splendor of the brick courtyard and looking up at the hardwood timbers of the pillars and roof joists.

"Canton is only sixty miles away," Lin laughed.

"I'm trapped in the lizard's tail," Jingyu told her.

"What?"

"You haven't heard the fable?"

"In Canton they keep the old tales from us."

"Once," began Jingyu, "China was dry and flat and inhabited only by great lizards. To prepare it for people, Shiva killed the lizards by cutting off their heads with a great sword. When the last of the great lizards fell, its tail became the seven villages, its spine the mountains, the blood from its neck the river, and the head Canton, with its mouth opening up into the sea."

Lin looked delighted.

"Its scales became plots of farmland and its spines turned porcelain. I know hundreds of old tales but they're all useless. That's why I say I'm trapped in the lizard's tail—the sixty miles to Canton might as well be six hundred."

"But you're a Mandarin. You've probably been in Peking and Shanghai."

"My parents were Mandarin, but they're dead. I was sent here to live with my uncle when I was hardly older than Peng."

"You sound like a well-educated Northerner."

"My uncle was a schoolteacher in Peking before he was sent here. He taught me what he could when he wasn't raising cabbages for the commune."

"Your husband is Mandarin too?" Lin asked.

"No, he's a Hakka. I think I'm about the only Mandarin in the seven villages. But haven't you ever heard my husband speak when he comes to get his teeth done? He has an accent that tilts words on their edges and even sends some of them teetering off into another language altogether."

Lin laughed, but managed to get out, "No, he goes to old Fu."

"That figures," Jingyu replied. "Fu is a Hakka too."

"And your new daughter is part Hakka now."

"I just hope she doesn't grow up to be as obstinate as Shang," Jingyu snorted.

"Your mother-in-law?"

"Yes. What do you think was the first thing she did when I brought home her first granddaughter this morning?"

"Probably try to look for a resemblance between Peng and her son."

"I wish. She started hitting me with sticks."

"Ah, one of those," Lin said, shaking her head. "With official policy limiting every family to one child, there'll be no male heir."

"Exactly," replied Jingyu.

"Horrors."

"Yes, horrors, but she really believes in that old stuff. When Kwang and I were first married she made three of the young neighbor boys sleep in our bed before us to implant a male image there. I know that things are very different in Canton, but here many people believe the same way as Shang."

"I thought that the People had stamped out that kind of repression."

"They stamped it out like vintage wine. They nurture it and store it away within themselves. On days like this they bring it out and get heady with it."

"Take her up before the Women's Association," Lin suggested.

"I don't think it'll go any farther than it has already," Jingyu said. "I gave her a piece of my mind before I left. Shang wants to be a good Communist, but there are too many of her ancestors living inside her. They're like locusts that prey on her good thoughts and leave her mind bare."

Just then, a woman wearing a sterile mask came to their table with a bowl of rice and vegetables for Jingyu. "Something for the little one?" she asked.

"Come back in several months," Jingyu laughed.

The worker took away Lin's bowl and went back into the kitchen. Lin, too, prepared to leave. "Watch out for your mother-in-law," she said. "I've read about some pretty fanatical old women in the *China Daily*."

"I think she is basically harmless," replied Jingyu. "Besides, my husband won't let her try any more funny stuff."

But when Jingyu returned home she found Kwang sitting slumped on the floor with his head in his hands.

"Kwang!" she cried. "What's wrong?"

Kwang looked up at her with deer's eyes, sad and wet. "I weep for my ancestors," he said. His forlorn gaze swept to a teak altar table on which stood portraits and photos of Kwang's forefathers.

Jingyu was concerned but also baffled. "Weep?" she thought. She moved over to the table and looked into the faces of the old men under glass. "What do your ancestors have to do with us?" she asked aloud. "Some of them probably went around with moldy rice in their beards for weeks at a time."

"Shh," he cautioned. "They will be angry."

"Let them, then," Jingyu said, but as she said it, a ghostly figure flew out of the next room with upraised sword. Jingyu screamed but then saw it was only old Shang, dressed in a flowing costume that probably would have been outdated in her grandmother's time and holding a hammer above her head. Jingyu barely managed to dodge the blow as the hammer descended onto the table, startling even Shang's ancestors, who shook in their frames.

"Blasphemy!" cried Shang in Hakka. "You shall be smitten and ground up by the People's new threshing machines for pig feed."

But, in truth, the hammer had slipped from her hand after her first swing, and all she could threaten Jingyu with was her wizened fist.

Jingyu picked up the hammer from the table and hefted it in her hand. "Ancestors?" she said. "Angry? How will they feel about this?" Carefully, she smashed the glass from one of the pictures of Kwang's forefathers. Shang screamed in pain and even Kwang's eyes and mouth flew open. "Please," he begged, but made no move to get up from the floor.

Looking at the faces of both her husband and his mother, Jingyu calmly and methodically smashed the glass from each of the small pictures, then threw the hammer down and left the room.

*   *   *   *   *

In bed that night, Kwang was conciliatory. "We can have other children," he said. "What can they do to us? Others do it."

"What if we have more girls?" asked Jingyu.

"Don't even breathe such thoughts," Kwang whispered.

"And how would it look to the Party?" asked Jingyu, disconcerted to feel the awakening of a part of her husband's body she wished would continue to slumber.

"We're not Party members," Kwang said.

"But we want to better ourselves, don't we?"

"Better ourselves how?" Kwang asked, inching closer to her so subtly he might have been a leech.

Jingyu wished she had leechlike powers too; then she could inch away again. "By moving away from the seven villages."

Suddenly, Kwang's progress stopped. "Why would we want to do that?" he asked, astonished.

"Listen, Kwang," she said excitedly. "In Canton they have restaurants from all cultures. They have shipments of new plastic raincoats. They have bon-bons and . . ." but Kwang cut her off.

"How does it concern us what they have in Canton?" he asked in a confused tone.

Jingyu moved closer to him in the bed. "I want to go to Canton," she said.

"We're poor," Kwang replied, turning over toward his side of the bed. "We can't even afford to buy new glass for the ancestors."

"We can join a cadre," she said. "I've heard that if we join a cadre they will send us to Canton, or even to Peking or Shanghai, to be educated."

"Forget it," he answered, taking her arm from around his chest and giving it back to her. "They will send you to Tibet to break rocks."

"They don't break rocks in Tibet," she said.

"How do you know?" he snapped, rolling over again to face her.

"I read it in a magazine Cao Lin lent me."

"I forbid it!" he said angrily, but Jingyu felt his body coming awake again.

"What?" she asked. "The magazine or the cadre?"

"I forbid it all! Now roll over. We're going to have another child."

"I forbid it," she replied.

*   *   *   *   *

Jingyu had left Peng at a day-care center and was having breakfast in the mess hall with Kwang and Shang. There were nearly a hundred others eating nearby, but the conversation was muted. To Jingyu it seemed as if everyone were saving their strength for work in the rice and cabbage fields. Everyone, that is, except Shang.

"I have given it a lot of thought," the old woman was saying. "And I have concluded that your bad actions yesterday were not wholly your fault."

"Whose, then?" Jingyu asked.

"The Gang of Four's," replied Shang.

"The Gand of Four are in jail," Jingyu pointed out.

"But their nasty thoughts pervade the country like a disease," said Shang. "Even in this temple." As the worker bringing their tea approached, Shang leaned forward and whispered, "There is a follower of the Gang of Four among us right now."

"Where?" Kwang asked, looking around.

"There," Shang hissed. "By the door."

Jingyu looked too, and saw Cao Lin chatting with another resident of her dormitory. Jingyu reached for her tea, but Shang pulled it away. "Look at her there," she commanded. "She was sent here for having Gang-of-Four ideas and now she will corrupt us all."

Jingyu gazed at Cao Lin for some moments, trying to convince herself that what Shang was saying couldn't possibly be true. But after all, even Jingyu didn't know why Lin had been sent to the seven villages. The clatter of a spoon falling to the table made Jingyu look away from Cao Lin. Shang had spilled tea on the table in her excitement and had a terrible gleam in her eye.

But Jingyu noticed that she also had white powder on her fingers and above the pocket of her jacket. "Cao Lin is a dedicated Party worker," Jingyu said, and again reached for her tea.

"She's a backbiter," hissed Shang. "And may all her children be dragons."

"She's not married," said Jingyu, noticing a residue of powder in the froth of her tea. She raised it to her face and smelled bitter almonds. "But maybe there's some truth to what you're saying after all. Perhaps I should take more care to please Kwang. Here, Kwang, have my tea. It's not right for a wife to be served before her husband."

Although Jingyu knew of no such custom, even among Hakka peasants, Kwang looked pleased, and reached for the cup she offered.

With a cry, Shang pointed and screeched, "Look!," and with her pointing finger, she knocked the cup from her son's hand.

Kwang looked where she pointed and, seeing nothing, looked at his mother in astonishment. "What's come over you?" he asked.

"Nothing," she replied hastily, rubbing her eyes. "I thought I saw a ghost—the ghost of your father—but it must have been the heat." She looked at Jingyu with daggers in her eyes.

Kwang looked at Jingyu more kindly and said, "Thank you anyway, Jingyu."

"Don't mention it," Jingyu told him.

*   *   *   *   *

Although she was still exempt by her maternity from going to work, Jingyu was getting antsy. As soon as Kwang and Shang left the table, she went looking for Cao Lin. She, too, had left the mess hall but Jingyu found her in front of her dormitory, doing Tai Ji Quan exercises with some of her housemates. Several of these women were members of cadres, and at least two were fairly high-ranking Party members sent from larger cities to help organize and educate the workers. In fact, Lin herself was a group leader who often led short discussions on the ideas of Chairman Mao. Cao Lin waved and smiled at Jingyu. "Come join us!" she shouted.

Jingyu was happy to comply. It had been weeks since she had taken any real exercise.

"How are you?" asked Lin, reaching her short fingers upward in imitation of a tree.

"Well," Jingyu replied, staring into inner space and trying to visualize clouds where there were none, "Shang tried to brain me with a hammer yesterday and poison me this morning, but I survived it.''

''You're kidding!'' Lin said in astonishment. She was now pushing out and pulling in her hands somewhat clumsily, as if trying to sculpt the tree.

Jingyu was more graceful. Her mind had created wisps of smoke, then vapors that her long and slender hands would shape into the clouds she sought. She loved Tai Ji, and gave herself up to it totally, clearing her mind even of the talk in the courtyard. As she twisted her body slowly this way and that, bent her knees carefully, and grew upward to the rhythm of pushing and pulling her cloud from place to place, she felt like she was not on a rice farm, but on a dance floor.

''Jingyu!'' Jingyu blinked and saw Lin standing in front of her with her hands on her hips. ''Come inside.''

Jingyu reached longingly for her cloud one last time, then followed Lin inside.

The dormitory—white, two-storied, and rectangular—was the largest building in the village. Lin's room was a mere cubicle, smaller even than the small bedroom Jingyu shared with Kwang. The bed, set against the wall, was a thin piece of matting inside a narrow frame. A sheet lay over the matting and mosquito netting was drawn away from both sides like curtains. A waist-high wooden bookcase held several revolutionary works, a few magazines and dental journals, and *Huckleberry Finn*. On another shelf stood two teacups and a flask for holding hot water.

''Where did you get *Huckleberry Finn*?'' Jingyu asked.

''In Canton,'' Lin replied. ''There's all sorts of foreign literature being published now. There are lines outside every bookstore. But tell me what your mother-in-law did.''

''I don't want to talk about Shang. I want to talk about Canton.''

''We'll talk about Canton later, now . . .'' but Jingyu interrupted her.

''How can I become a member of a cadre?'' she asked.

Lin pursed her lips. ''That's a serious question.''

''I'm not always scatterbrained,'' Jingyu replied.

"There's a lot of study involved . . ." Lin began.

"Well, look. I've studied all I can here."

"That's true, you'll have to go into a city. But what about your little girl?"

"She can visit day-care centers in the city."

"And it would get you away from Shang," Lin agreed. "Or would you be taking her with you?"

"Shang wouldn't want to leave the village of her ancestors," Jingyu replied.

"Still, she's become a dangerous woman. I'll talk to some of the Party members about you."

"You will?" Jingyu was delighted, especially since the idea of joining a cadre had popped into her head only a few hours ago.

"But don't get your hopes up."

It was too late. Jingyu was already running happily out of the dormitory. She wanted to tell Peng the good news.

That night, Shang seemed a changed woman. She cooed and cackled over Peng, although the little one was too young to respond. When Kwang came in griping about his tractor, which had broken down, and his co-workers, who had good-naturedly ribbed him about having to get his sandals wet in the soggy field, Shang just patted him on the arm and muttered sympathetically, "Gang of Four." In fact, she made up a little tune for Peng. "Gang of Four, Gang of Four," she sang.

Jingyu was astonished at the sudden change, but happy. Maybe now she could live her life without having to have each cup of tea chemically analyzed. She went to bed feeling better than she had in her life.

The room where she and Kwang slept had doorways to the other two rooms in the house. The first, an obsolete kitchen, had been remodeled into a bedroom for Shang. The other, the main sitting room, was where Peng slept in her bassinet. Jingyu kept the door open so she could hear Peng's slightest stirrings, but it was not a baby's cry that startled her awake that night; it was a clatter. A clatter, a patter, and a jiggle. Almost fully awake now, she heard Peng start to whimper. As she willed herself to get up, she heard shushing sounds. So Shang had decided to help her with Peng. How nice, she thought.

She raised herself to a sitting position and noticed that it seemed darker in the room than usual. No wonder; the door was closed. Perhaps that's what the clattering or the jiggling had been. She padded silently to the door and opened it wide, intending to thank Shang for trying to calm the baby, who was crying in earnest now. But in the moonlight that streamed through the window like the rays of a sun just being born, she saw Shang huddled against the wall looking guilty.

Jingyu flipped on the light. Shang was on her knees holding a wire, poised as if to plug in a lamp or radio. But, as Jingyu had already turned on the only light and they had no radio, Jingyu followed the line of cord to its source—the doorknob. The end of the wire had been snipped, stripped, and wrapped around the metal. If Jingyu had waited another three seconds before coming into the room, she would have been electrocuted. Shang looked up at her and smiled weakly. Jingyu screamed so loudly that she brought in not only her husband, but also a neighbor—a Party member who was quartered next to them while doing his annual month of volunteer labor.

The Party member, in his nightshirt, looked around the room, then spoke to Shang, who remained huddled on the floor with the plug still gripped tightly in her fist. "What have you got to say for yourself, Comrade?" he asked gravely.

"Gang of Four," Shang muttered.

*   *   *   *   *

That evening, Jingyu and Kwang were sitting across the room from each other in silence. Kwang was fiddling nervously with his hat. His face was haggard and unshaven. Jingyu was pouring hot water over green tea leaves. She had taken Peng to the day-care center while she tried to talk some sense into her husband. So far, nothing had worked.

"I should be at work," Kwang said, but he made no move to get up from the bamboo chair.

"Work has been over for an hour. Here, drink this."

Kwang shuddered, but took the cup she offered. "How can

I drink tea when my mother is being interrogated in some dungeon?''

"There are no dungeons in the seven villages," Jingyu replied. "They've just taken her to a happiness home."

"Where she will die!"

"Where she will be reeducated. If you are so concerned about her, why didn't you stop her from trying to kill me?"

"I'm sure she was just trying to shock you a little to make you see the error of your ways."

"And you agree with her methods, of course."

"A man must support his mother, if nothing else," Kwang replied defiantly.

"And you seem to be *doing* nothing else."

Kwang frowned at her. "You should never have had a girl-child."

"I see that now."

"It's all her fault."

"Her?" Jingyu said.

"Her. The girl-child. We were happy before."

"*You* were happy before, and her name is Peng. Xin Pengchi. And don't worry, she won't be around to bother you for long."

"She's sick?" asked Kwang with a mixture of concern and hope.

"She's going with me to Canton."

"Stop that stupid talk!" Kwang shouted. As an afterthought, he threw his teacup across the room to smash against the wall. Just then there was a knock on the door, and Cao Lin entered.

Kwang jumped up. "Where's my mother, and why won't they let me see her?" he demanded.

Lin stood in the doorway looking at the shards of teacup on the floor. She replied evenly, "Your mother has been taken to a rest home in one of the other villages—I won't tell you which one. You can see her in several weeks. Sooner, perhaps, because she seems no longer to be a danger."

"What do you mean?" Jingyu asked.

"It's odd, but Shang has *asked* for reeducation. She has confessed that what she did was reactionary and counterrevolutionary.

That sounds like rhetoric, but she really said it."

"You have hurt her," Kwang said.

"The People do not hurt one another," Lin answered.

Kwang picked up his large braided oval hat and strode toward the door.

"Where are you going?" Jingyu asked.

"I have some business to attend to," he said. "And there'll be no more talk about Canton! I want you to stay here until I come back!"

"Bind my feet, why don't you?" Jingyu replied.

Kwang slammed the door as he left.

Jingyu shrugged. "You see why I have to get away?" she asked.

"Get away?" Cao Lin sat down in the chair Kwang had just vacated.

"From Kwang. From the seven villages," Jingyu said.

Lin took off her glasses and polished them on the sleeve of her tunic. "You didn't tell me you want to go alone."

"I'm not going alone; I'm taking Peng."

"I don't know," Lin replied. "With Shang no longer a danger to you, some of the Party members feel you'll be of more use here—at least through the next harvest."

"But I don't want to stay for four or five months! Anyway, what makes you think Shang is sincere?"

Lin paused, then said, "Because I see in her something of myself."

"You?" Jingyu was taken aback.

"I volunteered for reeducation too."

"I didn't know."

"It's funny. You are anxious to leave your husband and work for the Party. I was just the opposite."

"You are married?" Jingyu asked. To hide her astonishment, she picked up another teacup and busied herself with wiping off dust motes. Then she filled it and handed it to Lin.

Lin took the cup. "He was my fiancé. I was very active in Party meetings and conferences, but when he was transferred to Shanghai, I wanted to leave everything I had and go with him."

"You could have begun again in Shanghai," Jingyu said. "There is no crime in wanting to be with someone."

"Perhaps not, but when I began begging the authorities to be transferred as well, my fiancé told me I must stay in Canton."

"Why?" Jingyu asked.

Lin took a deep breath and studied the broken pieces of the teacup on the floor. "He had another woman in Shanghai and was going there to marry her instead of me. He had not been transferred there by chance; he had asked for it. I should have known all along that he wouldn't want a homely woman. . . ."

"Those are reactionary thoughts," Jingyu said.

Lin's face took on an ironic smile. "Sometimes our attempts to leave the desert only bring us to the edge of the ocean. It makes you think to yourself, 'Now what?'"

Jingyu shrugged. "For me, I guess I'll go pick up Peng. Come with me."

"All right."

But when the two reached the day-care center, Peng was gone.

"Your husband picked her up already," the day-care worker told Jingyu.

Jingyu looked at Lin in a panic. "He has never even touched her before," she said.

"You think he may try to harm her?" Lin asked.

"He may do worse than that," Jingyu said.

"That's impossible," the day-care worker spoke up. "Killing infants is prohibited by Chapter 4, Article 13 of the Marriage Law."

"Which way did he go?" Jingyu asked impatiently.

"That way," the worker said. "Isn't that the way to your house?"

"The equipment shed," Jingyu said. With Cao Lin at her heels, she sprinted the two-hundred yards to the huge aluminum barn. A worker was strolling casually toward the mess hall, but otherwise there was no sign of life near the shed.

Jingyu ran up to the worker. "Have you seen Liu Kwang?"

she asked, trying not to let her alarm show.

"No. Wait a minute, I saw his tractor going toward the irrigation ditch about five minutes ago."

Jingyu, without waiting to catch her breath, turned toward the irrigation ditch and began running for all she was worth. The flat ground seemed to scoot out from beneath her feet as fast as she could put them down.

The irrigation ditch was a huge resevoir of water that would, in a month or so, be used to flood the rice fields. Jingyu could see it ahead, as well as the tractor, standing motionless. Beyond were mountains that looked so brittle they might fall away into shards of color at any moment. Jingyu was terribly out of breath, but managed to stagger to the tractor. Lin had arrived a few seconds earlier, and stood looking down the bank. Jingyu looked too.

Kwang sat with his hands in his hair. Just beyound, his great round wicker hat floated on the surface of the water. Inside the hat, wiggling and talking to herself, was Peng. She splashed the water with her tiny hand.

Jingyu leaned on the tractor with relief, then spoke. "Giving Peng a bath?" she asked.

Kwang looked up with a start. His face showed a rare despondency. His hair was disheveled and his hands were black with mud. "My ancestors will not be pleased with me," he said.

"Your ancestors are dead," Lin answered. "They lived their lives already; now you must live yours."

"Will Jingyu still go to Canton?" he asked Lin.

Lin looked at Jingyu, who scrambled down the bank and was fishing the round boat from the water. "She is free to do as she likes."

*   *   *   *   *

Jingyu and Kwang's house stood near the center of the last village in the seven village chain. With a strong basket containing her clothes, and a baby pouch strapped to her shoulders, Jingyu walked from one village to the next. When she arrived at the end of the first village in the chain she hitched a ride in a cart through the mountains. At the river she managed to beg standing room in a boat, whose owner gave her some fresh lentils and told baby jokes to Peng.

Two weeks after Jingyu and Peng left home, they arrived in Canton.

The Bowl of Sunshine

Amrita woke up and saw the train. It was hissing and blowing—a huge mechanical monster of iron and steel and steam. At first she was frightened. She thought she was having a nightmare and her lips began to quiver. But when she looked around for help, she saw hundreds of people rushing toward the train or milling around in small groups. Then she remembered: the railway station was her home now.

The famine had taken away their last few crops. Their ox had died and dust had come to take their land. Amrita and her mother and father had trekked into the city. They slept on the railway platform where it was warm and where they could build small fires and cook a meager dinner. There was no red dust in the railway station.

Amrita looked around the platform. All of the people clustered around her were poor. Their eyes were all hollowed out and their ragged clothing—torn and dusty from long days of begging on the streets—hung loose from their bodies. Like many of these people, Amrita and her parents could not afford shoes. That was all right with Amrita: she didn't like to wear shoes anyway.

Amrita lay back down on her bit of straw and smiled. She liked the bustle and the warm noise of the Bombay-Peshawar Express and the travelers and the many neighbors who slept beside her on the platform each night. Although she had not eaten in nearly 24 hours, she was glad to be alive and to have both her mother and father nearby. She only wished everyone could be as happy as she was. Everyone around her always looked so sad and acted so grumpy.

"Amrita, you lazy girl! Get up now! Get up!" It was her mother calling her, and Amrita scrambled to her feet. Her mother was squatting down in front of a small fire and boiling water. She had a small bowl of rice by her feet and she handed it to

Amrita.

"You eat it please, Mama," Amrita said. "I'm not hungry this morning." To Amrita, being hungry was just something else to get used to, like the many flies that hovered around the platform when there was food to be eaten. And indeed, Amrita's mother ate more than she did by far. She was a very big woman, but before the latest famine, she had been bigger. Now her face looked pained and her skin hung from her face and neck almost as loosely as her clothing.

"You're smaller than a dhyal bird," her mother answered angrily. "I want you to eat every bit of that rice."

Meekly, Amrita ate. It was just plain rice with a little sausage fat thrown in for flavor, but to Amrita it was like the finest gourmet dinner. She gulped it down in great mouthfuls.

"Amrita!"

Seeing her mother's disapproval, she realized that she was making a pig of herself, and ate more slowly.

Her mother nodded. "That's better," she told her. "But how many times must I tell you not to smile like that! We are poor. We have no more house, no farm. We have nothing. If the rich business people and travelers think that we are happy, they will give us no alms and we will starve."

"Yes, Mama."

"We have been living here for more than a month now, and still you will not remember what I have told you. Your father is on the street now, looking for food, or for some kind person who will help us with alms."

"I'm sorry, Mama," Amrita answered. "I'll remember now, I promise." All her life, Amrita had been told that she must obey her parents. It was tradition. It was what was taught in the schools. But Amrita's parents could no longer afford to send her to school.

"Do you also remember how I taught you to beg?"

"But Mama, I don't like to beg."

"Do you remember?" her mother demanded.

"Yes, Mama."

"Then go out to the square and see if you can get any money for once. You are young and thin and people will take pity on you if only you do as I tell you. Do you want your mother and father to starve to death?''

"No, Mama. I'll get something for us."

So Amrita went out of the station and into the street. It was so very hot that Amrita thought she was going to wilt like a flower. The red dust was thick in the air and she had to throw her shawl over her mouth and eyes until the small dust storm abated. All around her, men and women in fine business suits or exquisite saris hurried by on their way to work.

As she walked, Amrita saw several English visitors looking for the train station or for a cool hotel or cafe. She remembered what her mother had told her, but the English were so tall and they walked by her so fast that Amrita was afraid to ask them for any money. Some of them reminded her of bulldogs she had seen in picture books in school, or of frogs. The thought made her smile. But a smile would never do if she were going to bring back some money as she had promised.

Only then did she realize that she had forgotten her alms bowl. She looked around her at the other beggars standing with their backs to the hot stone buildings or slouched in doorways. They all had alms bowls. For most of them, it was their only possession. Some of the bowls had been made of clay, baked hard in the sun. Others were iron or tin in various states of wear: some were crimped or bent, others were rusted. Still, people put money in the bowls, or perhaps food, which the beggars ate quickly with their fingers. How was she going to beg if she had no bowl? Her mother would be very cross.

Maybe, she thought, she could find some old rice or beans behind some of the restaurants or cafes. She could wrap whatever she found in an old newspaper and carry it back that way. She knew that sometimes the restaurant owners would find rats or roaches in some of the food. Sometimes the food would be moldy or stale. Some, but not all of these owners would throw this moldy or rat-eaten food out. Amrita had once found some black rice and soggy bread in this way. She could wash or boil it later.

Suddenly, from nearby, she heard a faint moan. Was it a call for help, or was it a leper? She heard it again, louder this time.

She had to find out what was wrong. Maybe someone was hurt. It might even be her father. Someone might have beaten him up and taken away the money he had begged. The sound was coming from the other side of a low wall that separated the alley from an old deserted street. Amrita walked there cautiously and peered over the wall.

The sight that greeted her was a strange one, for on the other side of the wall lay an old holy man. Amrita knew he was a holy man because his beard was so long and his eyes gleamed so brightly as he looked up at her. Yet the old man was dressed in rags even more tattered than hers. His skin was tough and dark but he was as thin as a skeleton, and very weak. "What is the matter?" Amrita asked, but she didn't really have to ask. She had seen men in his condition all her life. "When is the last time you ate?" she asked him.

"I have touched no food nor drink in five days," the old man said in a slow, but gentle, voice. "If I could only have a small drink of water . . ."

Amrita noticed the man's bowl lying beside him. "Give me your bowl," she said, "and I'll bring you some water."

The holy one handed her the old and twisted tin bowl, but just the effort of reaching out made him gasp and nearly faint. Amrita was frightened and called out to a nearby restaurant owner to please come and help the old man. But the owner, a fat man, ignored her and walked back inside his restaurant. She called to a beggar who was going through trash cans, but he motioned her angrily away with his fist.

Amrita ran back out into the dusty main street. An ox was laboriously pulling a wooden cart through the street while his owner beat him with a whip. Amrita opened her mouth to ask the cart owner for help, but he raised his whip and would have hit her had she not jumped out of the way at the last second.

When the cart was gone, she looked around her, but all she saw were the hundreds of beggars who lined both sides of the street, trying to find a bit of shade for their parched skin. Suddenly, she saw a European man and woman come out of a restaurant. Immediately, a score of beggars set up cries of pain and hunger. Some began to move toward the European couple, but most were too hot and sick to bother. Amrita was young and very quick. She reached the couple ahead of the others.

"Please, sahib," she begged in her own language. "There is a holy man who is dying and needs something to eat. Can you carry him to a shady place and buy him a tiny bit of rice?" But the man was only a tourist and didn't understand a word of what she said. He drew a coin from his pocket and gave it to her with an angry look. "Here, beggar," he said. "Now leave us alone; all of you."

None of the beggars tried to take away the coin that she held so tightly in her fist. They even looked at her with a certain admiration for the way she had made the foreigner give up the money so easily. Could they think that she was one of them? A beggar? Then she realized that she was still holding the old man's alms bowl. It was only natural that the Europeans thought she was begging.

Amrita was so surprised that she had actually been begging that she almost gave the coin back. But then she remembered the old man. She went into the nearest cafe and asked for some rice and a cup of water. Only then, when she was paying for the rice, did she notice that the coin the man had given her was a very large one indeed. After she paid for the food she still had a lot of money left over. She tied up the money in her sari and hurried back to where the old man was lying.

The food and water helped, but the man was still much too weak to get up. She stayed with him much of the day, telling him about her family and many of the things she learned when she had gone to school.

"Every morning." she explained, "I and my friends would walk to a hut just outside of our town. Sometimes we would pick guavas and eat them for lunch or offer some to our teacher. The best times were when my father had to come into town to buy groceries. He would carry me on his shoulders and tell me how he wished that someday I could be a schoolteacher too. My father wasn't so sad then and my mother wasn't so stern." Amrita chattered away most of the day. Sometimes the old man smiled at her, but mostly he just dozed. Still, Amrita felt that she was help-ing him by staying. Later, on her way back to the railroad sta-tion, she bought a handful of rice so that her mother would not think she had been dawdling all day. She bought only a little, however, because she knew that without her help—and the help of the little bit of money she had left over—the old man would die.

For the next three days, Amrita visited the old man near the wall. She always brought him food, and the man seemed to gain strength day by day. Amrita combed his hair and beard and found ways to patch his torn clothing. "Why do you do this for me?" the old man asked.

"Because you are a holy man and because I have been taught to respect those who know more than I do." She laughed and said, "That means I have to respect just about everybody."

The holy man drew himself up and bowed to her. Though he was very old, his flowing hair and beard made him seem very regal. His eyes were like two crystals that could see far into the future. "It is I who respect you, child." he said. "Come with me. I have something to show you."

Leaning on Amrita only slightly, he led her down the dusty roads to the outskirts of town. On a path rarely used, Amrita saw a stone hut. It lay just outside a fence surrounding what used to be, in better times, a great temple. Now it was just a pile of ruins, and the fence was rotting. At the entrance to the hut, however, were three pilgrims, their heads shaved and their thick robes heavy with dust. They bowed to the ground as Amrita and the holy man approached.

"Come inside, child," the old man said. The inside of the hut was cool, for it was shaded by several mango trees. It was bare except for a sparse grass mat and several paintings of Vishnu on the walls. Amrita had expected the hut to be dark, because there were no windows. Instead, a gentle glow seemed to spring from somewhere inside the room. She noticed that the source of the light seemed to be coming from under the old man's sleeping mat.

"Little Amrita," the holy man began. "You helped me when no one else would. You have given me food when I would have starved without it. But most of all, you have given me hope and happiness with your chatting and your smile.'' And the old man told her a story.

"Many years ago, when I was a young student of the Holy Writings, I came upon a prince who had been beset by robbers and stabbed. The robbers ran away when they saw me, but the prince was dying. In his last breath he turned over to me a very curious and fearful object. 'You must not try to use it,' the prince told me, 'for I can see that you are only a carrier. But you must save it for the one who can.' 'But how will I know who that one is, my lord?' I asked. 'You must study,' he said, 'And then you will know.' Then the prince died, and vanished before my eyes. I have studied the Holy Writings all my life, but I have never seen a single mention of the beautiful object he gave me. Although I do not even know what it is used for, I have kept it for you all these years.''

"For me, holy one?'' Amrita gasped.

"Yes, for I know now that you are the one for whom I have been keeping it. You are the one the prince spoke of.'' And as the old man finished speaking, he lifted his straw-filled mat and from under it, in a shallow hole, he took out a gleaming golden bowl. It was bright—like a little sun—and Amrita knew that it was the source of light for the dim little hut. She took the object in her hands and admired it.

"Why, it's a bowl of sunshine,'' she said happily.

The old man chuckled and said, "Yes, child, so it is. A bowl of sunshine.''

"But how is it to be used?'' she asked.

"Only you will know that,'' the holy man said. "And likewise, you will be the only one who will know who you must give it to when you are through with it. I only know that it cannot be used for food or for begging, for what you have in your hands is the food of life. With it, you will be the giver, not the taker. And often you may have to give to those who think they do not want what you are offering them. What you have, little one, must be given freely. It cannot be taken away from you. Go now.''

"But what about you?'' cried Amrita. "You will starve, and I have no more money to help you.''

"You have helped me all you can. Outside, there are three that have come for me. I must journey to the mountains with them, and I will be provided for."

"What will you do in the mountains?" asked Amrita. She was sad because she felt that she would never again see the old man she had become so fond of.

"I think perhaps, little one, that I am going there to see my prince."

"Goodbye, holy one," Amrita said.

"Goodbye, child."

Amrita soon found herself alone on the road back to the Bombay railroad station. She held the marvelous, shining bowl in her hands and she stared at it in curiosity and awe. It was the most beautiful thing she had ever seen, but what was she to do with it? And why had she, a young girl, been entrusted with the keeping of it? Strangely enough, Amrita felt that the bowl was truly hers and that, indeed, it had always been hers. With the bowl in her hands Amrita was no longer aware of the bad odors coming from the steaming hot city. She no longer noticed the great billows of red dust that swirled by her like a storm of hot pepper.

Suddenly, from a ditch beside the road, a thief ran up to her with a knife and a menacing, evil leer. "Give me that golden bowl," he demanded, showing his dirty teeth as he spoke. Amrita looked around for help, but she was not yet in the city and the road was deserted.

"No!" Amrita cried. "You mustn't take it." But the man was already reaching for it. Just as Amrita was sure the bowl would be snatched from her, the thief gave out a loud scream and fell to the ground.

"You burned my hand!" he cried angrily, getting back to his feet and brandishing the curved knife at her. He raised the knife to strike her but, all at once, the air was filled with so bright a glowing white light that the thief was temporarily blinded. The light terrified him and, with a loud cry, he staggered away into the ditch. To Amrita, the light was just a warm and comforting glow. She marveled at the power she held in her hands.

Hesitantly, she put her fingers into the bowl and felt a tingling as the light rays danced back and forth along the smooth sides. It was a nice sensation and Amrita smiled. When she took her hand back out, some of the rays were still clinging there.

Back in the railway station, Amrita's mother was sitting on a pile of rags holding a pot. She was waiting for the next train to come in so she could sneak into the lavatories of the high-class sleeping compartments for a bit of pure water to cook with. When she saw Amrita she scowled and demanded, "What little bit did you manage to get today?"

Amrita had completely forgotten about food or alms, and she was ashamed. "Nothing, Mama. I forgot."

"You forgot, did you? Maybe if I give you a good beating you won't forget any more! What's that you have? A new alms bowl? Where did you steal it?" As Amrita's mother got closer to the bowl her mouth dropped open in astonishment. "Why, that bowl is pure gold," she breathed.

"Please, Mama," said Amrita quickly. "Don't touch it."

"Give me that bowl. Owwww, it's hot!" she screamed. "It's burning!"

Her mother's reaction to touching the bowl sent Amrita tumbling backwards, where she put out her hand to steady herself and touched several beggars who were looking on. Because most of the beggars she had met were a surly bunch, Amrita expected them to give her a smack or two on the ears. Instead, she saw that the beggars were smiling at her kindly. "Don't be nasty to the little girl," one of them said to Amrita's mother. "You should be more charitable to her," said another.

"What do you beggars know about charity?" Amrita's mother demanded.

The first beggar, a thin, starved-looking man with a pinched face, said, "I know only that each of us is poor through no fault of our own. Our crops have failed, our cattle have died, and a desert of dust has taken over what used to be our fields. We have good reason to feel sad and even desperate. Only your daughter has kept her happiness with her through these bad times. She cheers us up, she gives us hope that maybe tomorrow things will be better than today."

A woman spoke up: "If she can remain happy in such a place as this, then perhaps the rest of us should benefit from her example."

"Why have you never spoken like this before?" Amrita's mother asked suspiciously.

The beggars said nothing more, but Amrita knew why. Her hand, with its clinging rays of sunshine, had brushed the beggars as she tried to regain her balance. Now she knew the secret of the bowl of sunshine. "Look, Mama," she said, and dipped her hand once more into the bowl.

"You stay away from me with that bowl," Amrita's mother said, backing away from her. "Go get rid of it. Sell it somewhere."

As Amrita brushed her mother's sari, the older woman fell backwards over a pile of clattering cooking utensils, her face a mixture of sadness, anger, and fright. When she looked up, however, she was smiling. It was the first smile Amrita had seen on her mother's face in many months.

It was a strange sight that greeted Amrita's father when he came back to the railway station after begging for many hours in the heat and terrible dust. Everyone on the platform was milling around, chatting, smiling, and patting one another on the back. And it was not only the beggars who were doing this, but also the European travelers and the rich, fat, Bombay business people who were usually so rude to everyone. And in the center of the crowd he saw his daughter, Amrita, talking excitedly to the station manager, who listened to her as if what she had to say was very interesting indeed. Then he noticed that his daughter held an odd-looking bowl that gave off a golden glow. He wondered what it was, and what was in it.

Smiles?

The Man Who Wrote Letters to Comic Books

At midnight Oz Crockett tosses down the last of his Olympia beer and drops the can on the floor of the Malamute Saloon. On a rough stage near the bar, the Alaskan Hillbillies are punching out a Waylon Jennings tune. Like Oz, they are in their mid-forties and balding. Like him too, their movements are rote and wooden. On the way to the door, an old Native hits him up for a cigarette. That's all right; he has plenty.

Outside, 4th Ave. foams with a slow activity. Men and women move like glaciers across the row of bars and pawn shops. These others—mostly old timers or Natives transplanted from small villages along the Arctic Circle—do not feel the bitter cold. They drift from one bar to the next with the cautiousness of hunters wearing snowshoes. Oz Crockett has never gotten used to the cold and he shifts his hands into his down jacket. His home is not far away, but he shuffles more quickly than the others. Along with the down jacket the color of tobacco stain, he wears patched coveralls several sizes too large and old hiking boots laced with twine. The bill of his cap points his way.

His home is an anachronism, constructed entirely of oak logs and nearly surrounded by a modern apartment complex. A dozen blocks away, the Captain Cook Hotel flashes its red light like a looming beacon to warn Oz Crockett that the new building looks ready to eat the small cabin. Everything in Anchorage, he thinks, is hungry.

Inside, he kicks off his boots and extracts two objects from his back pocket, a copy of the *Tundra Times* and a comic book. He flicks on a light and checks the stove. Although he has electricity, he still prefers the heat from a wood stove. He adds four logs to the smoldering coals and sits down at a large desk constructed from an old door and some logs. It tilts toward him slightly like a drafting table. On the floor beside him are stacks of comic books, a sheaf of filler paper, several pens, and a pair of spectacles. He puts on the glasses, picks up a piece of paper, and begins to write.

Dear Editor,

I just bought a copy of Dazzler #5. It's a decent book despite a couple of pages of shoddy pencilwork. If you're not going to do it all good, then do it all bad; that way nobody will know that your standards are askew. As for Dazzler herself: her powers are unusual enough to attract an audience, and her dialogue is the best since Spider-man's. That's why it's so tragic that you choose to continually pit her against world-eaters and galaxy-gobbling super enemies. Give her a break. You don't have to look into fantasy to find things to combat. There're enough in every city on earth to keep any superhero busy for a lifetime. Get with it. Characters like Dr. Doom and the Enchantress are stupid (except on theological and mythological levels). Go back to your roots. Look at the earliest Superman. He fought plain flesh-and-blood criminals. The worst problems imaginable are right here and right now.

I haven't seen any sign of my latest suggestion—Seal Woman. In fact, none of my ideas have had any success lately. Still, my latest character is irresistible. I call him the Tippler.

*   *   *   *   *

The Tippler, #1: Origin

Ozwald Crockett was born in Kentucky, near the same part of the woods where his great ancestor Davy became a legend. He was an average boy who inherited his mother's love for art and his famous ancestor's interest in politics. His father disappeared when he was very young, and his mother had all she could do just to eke out a slim living doing advertisements for a small department store in Frankfort. Ozwald had to be satisfied with a small community college education that taught him only the rudiments of the art he longed to create. His paintings were quick failures, and after he graduated he felt lucky to catch on with a small newspaper as an incidental illustrator. In time he was able to contribute a weekly cartoon strip on the evils of whatever political party happened to be in the news at the time. It didn't matter which party it was because, although his cartoons always started out as biting satires, they came out confused, as if Oz were never sure what was being lampooned and what was not. He knew that he was not a good illustrator and that his cartoon was mediocre, but he did his best and often wished that his best were better.

One day he was called into his editor's office—a spacious room with glass walls. The editor was a ruddy-faced man who had once worked for a large Washington newspaper.

"Oz," he began. "I'm going to have to take you off the payroll."

"What?"

"We're going to a new format and I don't think we should stay with the same illustrator."

"But I've been here for ten years," he said.

"I know that, and I feel bad about it. You should have known this was coming, though."

"You mean when you hired Randy to do my work."

"Not to do your work, Oz; to help you out."

"So now I *am* out?"

"Yes. Randy's just too good."

"But where am I going to get another Job?" Oz said with dismay. "All the other papers have good artists already."

"That's the real problem, Oz: you're not a good artist. You leave too much to the imagination. Since Randy's been with us our circulation has gone up seven percent. That's seven percent in just three months, Oz. That says something to me. Look, maybe I can find a job for you taking classifieds or in circulation."

"You mean delivering a route, don't you?"

"It's not a bad job."

"What about my strip?" Oz asked.

"It's not a good strip, Oz. It never was. Readers have been grumbling about it for months now. I asked you to tone it down a long time ago but you wouldn't listen. Look, Oz, politics is too volatile to go stabbing away at it like some grotesque version of blind man's bluff. You should have invented Dagwood or something."

"But I love politics."

"Next time you love something, be kinder to it."

Oz Crockett walked out of the office in a deep gloom. He knew it would be impossible to get a job on another newspaper as an artist. Maybe he would take up the offer of a route. No, his love was for art and for politics, not for newspapers. Oz felt queasy. For all his working years he had everything he wanted. Now—suddenly—he had nothing.

He had a bit of money saved up; maybe he should do some traveling. But where should he go? The answer came quickly in the form of a letter from a lawyer in Alaska. Oz Crockett's long-lost father had died in Anchorage several weeks before. Would Mr. Oz Crockett care to fly to Anchorage to discuss the matter?

*　　*　　*　　*　　*

Oz Crockett puts down the pen and runs his writing hand through his whitening beard. The Tippler wasn't working out. It was taking him too long to get to the action.

He unfolds his newspaper. There are two major newspapers in town—one, the *Daily News*, is a liberal, general interest paper with high journalistic standards. The other, the *Anchorage Times*, represents big business in the state. That means the oil companies. Oz Crockett reads the *Tundra Times*, a Native newspaper. Although he likes the oil companies, he also likes their arch-enemies the conservationists. There is substance for a comic book there somewhere, and Oz Crockett makes a mental note to suggest a series of some kind to DC. But that isn't the reason he likes them. He likes them because together, like two black clouds colliding to cause a thunderhead, they create a political situation. Oz Crockett feels the warmth of the wood stove reaching out toward his chair. It has been more than fifteen years since Oz Crockett lost his first and last job, but he still loves politics. His cartoon strip may have been a dud, but he still enjoys the barbed cartoon. The *Tundra Times* is also full of grist. Alaskan Natives want state lands, the conservationists want federal lands, and the oil companies want to take all the land away from both groups. Good for them. All of them. Oz Crockett thinks that in his prime he could have whipped off an easy bit of satire. He can even picture it in his mind: a Conestoga wagon driven through Eskimo country by an oil rig and a gas pump. The wagons are drawn by a team of Chevrolets, and the Eskimos are throwing harpoons from dog sleds, etc. It would be easy to draw. The problem is this: Oz Crockett still does not know who is right. Who is the butt of the satire? The conservationists? The oil companies? Who is right and who is wrong? These days, all his ideas are like that. He puts the newspaper aside.

Outside, the snow has begun drifting down like tiny pieces of lint. He crumples up the paper he has been writing on and throws it in the stove. But instead of getting up, he starts writing again.

*   *   *   *   *

The Tippler, #1 (continued)

Oz Crewcut, former bad political cartoonist, came to Anchorage to avenge his father's death. His father had disappeared just after Oz was born, but Oz learned that he had worked his way to Alaska to become first a homesteader, then a Native Claims organizer. He was found just a week before Oz arrived, frozen to death in the Chugach Mountains, five miles outside the city.

It had been a great shock. He had used the last of his money to fly 3,000 miles. Now he had no job and no father.

"I'm glad you could come," said the burly, dark-haired lawyer.

"It seems pointless," Oz had replied. "My father's dead."

The lawyer, who had introduced himself as Barney Barnett, ran a thick hand along his ebony hair and leaned back in his swivel chair. "Your father left a will," he said. "He left everything he owned to you."

"But he hardly knew I existed," Oz protested bitterly. "He left my mother when I was a baby."

"He knew. And I think he wanted to make up for that."

"It's way too late," Oz said.

"I suppose anyone in your situation would be bitter," said Barney Barnett. "But your father was a complex man, and when you get to know his memory better, I think you'll realize that he was also a good one. He didn't have much to leave: just a log cabin. But it was built before Anchorage was hardly even a city, and the property it occupies is worth a bundle."

"I don't need the money," Oz lied.

"Live in it, then."

"Live in Alaska?"

"There are worse places."

"How long have you lived here?" Oz asked.

Barney Barnett laughed. "Maybe you think this dark skin is from a month in Acapulco. I was born in Barrow. Can't you recognize an Eskimo when you see one?"

"How could I?" Oz stammered.

"Mr. Crockett, we liked your father."

"How did he die?"

"He killed himself," Barney Barnett reported.

Oz Cronkite was shocked numb. His body felt cold and so rigid he couldn't even shiver. "Killed himself?" he said.

"He turned his back to the city and walked as long as he could into the mountains."

"Why?" Oz forced himself to ask.

"Come with me and I'll show you," Barney Barnett said.

Continued, 2nd page following

*   *   *   *   *

The fire is getting too warm and Oz Crockett pushes the damper of the stove all the way back. His interest in comic books is more than that of a failed old cartoonist to a successful strip, and his interest isn't new. He has always been attracted to the fantasy in life—the myriad worlds where everyone's hopes and dreams may and often do come true. To worlds where winos and derelicts can build beauty and muscle out of once-dismal clay. His father had once had a dream and it had not panned out. Perhaps his father and he were alike.

Sometimes when Oz returns home from 4th Ave., he has drunk enough so that he does not feel hunger. Tonight is different, and he opens a package of crackers and a tin of sardines. He puts a pot of coffee on the stove. His dinner table is a huge spool that the utilities company left after they strung up his neighborhood with electricity. Eating the crackers and sardines, Oz Crockett finishes reading his newspaper. Sometimes Oz Crockett finds his own name in the *Tundra Times*—a great distinction for a white man.

Oz Crockett's mind wanders. White Man, who can change the course of racial harmony, bend minds with his bare hands . . .

When Oz Crockett first came to Alaska he tried to create his own comic books. He even sent his ideas to Marvel and DC with his resume (much inflated, but who would ever check?), but they were always returned. Oz hadn't expected anything. They, too, were shoddy pieces of work. His only success was Ice Man, who had the ability to freeze any object around him, even the molecules in the air. But Ice Man had been appropriated for a comic that had nothing to do with Alaska, and Oz Crockett never thinks of him as his creation. The few dollars a month in residuals, however, keeps Oz in cigarettes. He lights one now and takes a tin cup of coffee back to his work table. He has time to finish his episode before he goes to bed.

*   *   *   *   *

The Tippler, #1 (continued)

The place Barney Barnett took Ozwald Cocktail was a dingy bar called the Montana Club. It was one of a streetful of similar saloons interspersed with a pawn shop here and a porno shop there. Doors between saloons led upstairs to dimly lighted hotel rooms.

Men and women with long slick hair and rounded cheekbones passed like shadows from one bar to another or slouched in doorways. No one paid any attention to Oz Crackpot or Barney Barnett; they seemed to be occupied in private conversations or solitary thoughts.

"These are my people," Barney Barnett began, as he led Oz to a rough wooden table near the back wall. "They're mostly Natives, and they're all incurable boozers. Some are only in their teens and the ones that look sixty are really only thirty. They come here because they have no place else left. Big business has bought their land, replaced their food, and made their customs obsolete."

"Where do they live?" Oz Condo asked.

"Here. They sleep right here in the doorways, or out back. Or if they happen to have a few bucks, upstairs with the rats."

"Can't they get on welfare or something?" Oz asked.

"They *are* on welfare. That's what this is all about." Barney Barnett was interrupted by a slim, thirtyish, bleached-out waitress who took their orders for beer and slipped back behind the bar. "Thirty-five years ago," Barney Barnett went on, "Eskimos were content to live in their villages, but when the oil companies spread like smallpox all over Alaska, it was as if the state turned a sickly, greenback green overnight. Suddenly Eskimos had money to buy snowmobiles that were stronger and faster than huskies. There were guns and rifles so powerful they could split a walrus' skull from so far away you could hardly see the white tusks, and there were Big Macs that you didn't have to spend hours lying face down on the ice in zero-degree weather to catch. The life they've tried to lead for centuries has vanished like ice brought to the desert."

The beer came, and Barney Barnett took half of it down in one tip. Oz Cognac, who liked to drink, sipped his more slowly.

"I come here a lot," Barney Barnett went on. "I recognize the illness, but I come here anyway, like a cancer victim lighting up, or like a one-armed man returning to the sausage factory."

"But what is it? What is this place?" Oz Crocus bent forward and looked around the bar. It was very dark but he could make out two darker-skinned men shoving each other near a pool table. An older, more ponderous couple swayed together to a not-quite-clear jukebox song, in a grotesque parody of an embrace.

"This is the pits you hear about so often. It's the place elephants come to will their tusks to fortune seekers. I never came here when I was younger. I went to college and to law school because I was real gung-ho about leaving this kind of legacy behind. But all I've done is take on someone else's culture. You can't leave legacies behind. There's something about having your entire history erased that gets to you. I come here to drink with my people. It's the only experience we can share any more. After I've had a few it doesn't seem to matter that the Eskimos are doomed as a people; it doesn't matter that I've run out on my race. If I'm in enough of a haze I can pretend that everything is still real." Barney Barnett held his empty beer bottle up to the light. "Join me?" he asked.

"Sure."

At the end of three hours, Oz Crocked nearly forgot about his father.

When he remembered, he was much too drunk to ask, or even remember, the right questions, but he learned two things anyway. He learned about despair and invulnerability. The despair was in the lines of every crumbling face he saw, and the invulnerability was in the alcohol. He slept on a couch in Barney Barnett's office that night, and although he stumbled into chairs and tables like a cowpoke in a saloon gunfight, although he fell headlong onto the marble floor in the middle of the night, he felt nothing. He had become the Tippler.

Next, The Roughneck

*   *   *   *   *

Oz Crockett lays down his pen. Still no damn good, he thinks. No action at all. Just drivel. Oz Crockett walks to his bed and falls into it. He is asleep in minutes.

Oz Crockett wakes up with a surge of purpose just before noon. He splashes water on his face, heats up the pot of coffee, and uncovers a battered old typewriter. With his mug of coffee nearby, he bangs out the following letters.

Bloodstone Const. Co.
340 N. D St
Anchorage, AK   99501

Dear Mr. Bloodstone:

This is to inform you that unless you cease plans to start landfill operations adjacent to the property of Joseph K. Berengetuk, we will be forced to ask our solicitor to take legal action against you because of the drainage problem it will cause Mr. Berengetuk.

Sincerely,
O. Crockett, for Native Claims

Exxon Corp.
770 W. 5th Ave.
Anchorage, AK   99501

Dear Personnel Mgr:

I am writing this letter on behalf of Will Minolomung
of Nuiqsut, who was laid off of his job at your camp near
Prudhoe Bay on Thursday last. As you know, this is in
violation of Mr. Minolomung's rights as an area Native.
Unless you reinstate Mr. Minolomung by return mail,
we will be forced to turn the matter over to our solicitors.
       Thank you for your kind attention to this matter.
                         Sincerely,
                         O. Crockett, for Native Claims

Native's rights. Well, thinks Oz Crockett, at least they still have
some rights. The only problem is that both Joe Berengetuk and
Will Minolomung are full-time drunks. Oz Crockett, who is only
drunk three-fourths of the time, has to act for them. He looks
out the window and notices that it is snowing fiercely. There are
several bottles of Olympia on the windowsill for just such occasions, and he takes one down and twists off the cap. Breakfast.

His handwritten pages of the night before are still on his
worktable. He picks them up and reads them carefully. Pretty
bad, but practice makes perfect, and Oz Crockett has been prac-
ticing for fifteen years. He slips another piece of paper into the
typewriter and begins typing.

*   *   *   *   *

The Tippler, #2

The Tippler awoke one morning covered with snow. Since he had
discovered his invulnerability, he slept often in doorways or alleys off
4th Ave. He was slowly getting used to his new life. A jackhammer was
going off in his head and he looked around for the source. Nothing. The
streets were white and clear in the dawning light. Where was the noise
coming from?

Then, blocks away, the Tippler saw stick figures coming toward him. Each twiggy step sounded in his head. So. He had superhearing too. The figures were moving frantically toward him. A shout rang through his ears like a pistol shot. One man was chasing another, and it looked serious. The sidewalk was icy, and though neither of the men fell, each slipped and slid with almost every step. Then the Tippler, from his mound of snow against the wall, saw the flash of a knife as the men came closer. Something had to be done, so as the first man picked his way past him in terror, the Tippler hunched up, scattering snow everywhere as he flapped his arms. The second man—the man with the knife—was startled as he saw our hero hunker up from nowhere. But the Tippler slipped down again, causing the man to go hurtling over his body and slide face forward on the icy sidewalk.

The Tippler had struck. The impact would have hurt a normal person, but the Tippler had made his skin numb. He got up and staggered toward the man, who had dropped his knife and was lying face down on the sidewalk, sobbing into the melting ice. The first man had turned a corner and was out of sight.

"What's wrong, pal?" The tippler helped the man to his feet.

"Who are you?" asked the man, who turned out to be quite a big man indeed. His beard was red, like his down jacket, and he was wearing a yellow Sohio cap. The Tippler knew the man was a roughneck—a rig man.

"A friend." the Tippler replied. "Why don't we go into that cafe over there and have some coffee and you can tell me why you wanted to kill that man."

"Why should I?" the roughneck asked with a tearful show of belligerence.

"Because I'll listen," the Tippler replied. "And no one else will."

Continued, 2nd page following

*   *   *   *   *

Oz Crockett stops typing and puts a couple of logs in the stove. That's the trouble, he thinks. There's no one else to do a lot of things. Inept letters to big corporations, silly letters to comic books. He knows he doesn't have to write them, but if he doesn't, who will? And if he doesn't, what would he do instead? That's the big problem, how to get through the day. Oz Crockett, who has steadfastly refused to answer that question, even to himself, starts typing again.

*   *   *   *   *

"My name is Mike Hutto," said the roughneck in the cafe. He stopped for a moment and warmed his hands on his coffee cup. He took a biscuit from a plate on the table. The Tippler hoped the roughneck had some money. By a little furtive exploration, he found that someone had relieved him of his change during the night. The Tippler was glad to help.

"I work at Pingo, up on the Slope. I help change drill bits and do a little clean-up work besides. I'm usually at the camp two weeks at a time, then I fly back here for two weeks. But that's no way to live."

The Tippler made a guess. "You're married?"

The roughneck hung his head. "Yeah. But how can you have a marriage when the only time you can see your wife is when you're tired from the cold and the work and wild for any kind of diversion at all? When I come home I'm either asleep or out at a restaurant or watching a movie or out buying stuff. Cindy and I never get much of a chance to talk. I came home this morning unexpected—I was pretty sick up at camp—and caught her with some bozo."

"That was the man you were chasing?"

"Yeah."

"And you were going to kill him?"

"It would have been better than killing myself."

"My father killed himself," the Tippler said.

"Oh yeah? What for?"

"I don't know. He walked into the mountains Eskimo style."

"Eskimos have strange ways of doing things. Me? I'll just shoot myself in the head. I don't like the cold, you know?'

"I'm glad you can kid about it," the Tippler said. "It means you're probably going to be all right."

"What do you know about it?" the roughneck asked.

"I spend a lot of nights in bars and I see a lot of guys like you. You're taking it better than most. At least you know the reasons behind it. You'll be all right."

"Maybe I will."

After the man paid and left (the Tippler tried to stay in the warm room but was shooed out like a fly), the Tippler turned back into Ozwald Cream-puff, wealthy landowner, and walked the few blocks to his cabin. After lighting a fire, his mind began going over the events of the morning. A woman becomes lonely and starved for conversation because her hus-band is too tied up in his work. She becomes vulnerable to other men. . . . Start again.

A lonely city man looks for companionship but finds that most of the women who interest him are married to men that work in the camps. Eventually he is attracted enough to begin talking to one of these women and finds her to be excellent company, and strangely responsive to him. . . . Start again.

A camp worker goes after the big money by staying 300 miles away from civilization for weeks at a time. He becomes well-to-do, and is able to buy almost anything he or his wife needs, but the work drains his body and starves his senses. Back in the city everything seems unreal. His wife is like someone on the TV screen. . . .

These three pictures made Ozwald Copout wince. Could nothing be done? And who was to blame? Maybe the roughneck understood the reasons behind it, but Ozwald hadn't a clue. With resignation and a lit-tle horror, he realized that no one was to blame. It was a condition of the life they led. A condition of their own making. It was a bitter Alka Seltzer for Ozwald Cachet to swallow. What about his own father's suicide? As the Tippler, he still searched every day for information about his father's death, hoping that mitigating circumstances might assuage some of the animosity he still held on to. But what if no one was to blame there either? It was depressing, and Ozwald Conehead longed to make his mind a blank. He needed to forget about all this—to use none of his faculties. He needed, in fact, to change back into the Tip-pler, and he wondered if the bars were open yet.

*　　*　　*　　*　　*

Like his creation, Oz Crockett doesn't want to think, but sometimes he has no choice. He's rarely morbid, but sometimes it flashes into his head like the gleam of a knifeblade that he is 46 years old. And what has he accomplished? Status as a usually tipsy volunteer for Native Claims? Barney Barnett had fled to the United States to escape his destiny, but before he left he had roped Oz Crockett into assuming his father's role. Now the rest of his father's fate is creeping up on him like the shadows of the mountains overlooking the city. It's this Tippler business, carrying him back to places he doesn't want to return to.

The snow has escalated into a full-fledged storm, and what little light there was is starting to vanish. He has almost made it through another day. He opens another bottle of Olympia from the windowsill and picks up his pen.

> Dear Marvel,
>
> I like your character Wolverine because he, more than any other superhero, has a killer's lust. Of course the Comics Code doesn't allow a superhero to kill, but I appreciate your bringing to the forefront an urge that most people would have if given the situation and the opportunity.
>
> You missed a bet, though. A wolverine's fur is hollow; each strand is insulated. If Wolverine lived on the North Slope, he could go for days without warmth. But of course you have a hero in Alaska already: the Tippler.

*　　*　　*　　*　　*

The Tippler, #3

It was a stormy, snowy night, and Ozwald Coldcut prepared to leave his cabin and drift out into the darkness . . .

*　　*　　*　　*　　*

Oz Crockett puts down the pen. He has written too much already. Night is falling and, although the snow is still coming down like heavy static, it is time to go out.

On goes his down jacket, his boots, his cap. He trudges through the snowy streets head down, hands in his pockets. It takes him longer than usual to walk the several blocks. When he arrives, however, 4th Ave. is alive and aglow with people trapped in a snowy paperweight—a colony of beings who move slower than humans.

Oz Crockett slouches into the Montana Club and sits at the bar. There is no live music tonight so the sounds of conversation and arguing are louder than usual. One voice in particular stands out. It sounds vaguely familiar, a combination of Innupiat and New York drawl. Oz Crockett looks into the corner and sees Barney Barnett, who is talking to another Native in a far corner of the bar. He is obviously and obliviously drunk. When the other man moves away, Oz Crockett takes his beer to Barney Barnett's table and sits down.

"Crockett, you old hero." Barney Barnett's cheeks have rounded even more than they had been before. He has put on about 50 pounds and is bloated. His suit is expensive but wrinkled, as if he has been wearing it for days. His eyes have sunk a bit in his head, but he looks glad to see Oz Crockett.

"Why did you come back?" Oz Crockett asks almost sadly.

"Why do lemmings run into the sea?" Barney Barnett replies.

"I don't think lemmings really do that," Oz Crockett says.

"Why do salmon swim up into the Kenai River when they know that the canneries have extinction privileges?"

"That's not the same thing."

"Have a beer," says Barney Barnett.

"I have one now."

"Have another. Have two or three. What have you been doing for the last few years?"

"Nothing much. I've grown a beard and gotten a few years older. I've written a few letters for Native Claims."

"I've heard. Much success?"

"Some, maybe."

"Fourth Avenue is still here."

"That might be a good thing."

"For you or us Eskimos?"

"It gives us all somewhere to go."

"Instead of for a walk in the mountains, eh?"

"You're too drunk to talk."

"Look, Crockett," Barney Barnett says loudly, "I've longed to take that last walk a thousand times. In Tucson, in New York, in Palm Beach. In Acapulco."

"So you came back here to help?"

"I don't know why I came back." Barney Barnett finishes one beer and starts another. "Yes I do, too. I came back to find my heritage, whatever that means. I came back to . . ." He stops, confused.

"To help," Oz Crockett repeats.

"Have it your way. I couldn't let you bear the whole brunt."

"We all bear it," Oz Crockett says.

"But you bear it without feeling it. You carry the cross and you're not even a goddam Christian."

"But I do feel it," Oz replies. "My heritage is here too. My father died here for something he believed in."

"You'd like to believe that, wouldn't you?"

"Everybody has to believe in something."

"Your father died because he was losing his own heritage. He ran out on his family and on the only other people who ever needed him."

"You don't know that." Oz Crockett says.

"Of course I know it. Look, man, your father was guilt-ridden as hell for leaving you and your mother. Why do you think he threw himself into Native Claims like he did?"

"Why?" Oz Crockett asks.

"Because he saw the Eskimo people as proxies for you."

"Why didn't he come back to Kentucky, then?"

"Why don't the Eskimos kick Exxon out of their villages?"

"Why?"

"That was a rhetorical question and rhetorical questions don't require answers."

"So why did he kill himself?" Oz Crockett was drinking too fast and the beer was making him slow; why else would he keep asking why over and over again?

"You don't think I know the answer to that either, do you? But I do know. He killed himself so he could give you your legacy."

"What legacy?"

Barney Barnett flings his finger around the room. "This!" he shouts. "This bar, this strip, this despair."

"Why not just will it to the Eskimos?" Oz asks.

"They have it already, but theirs is one-way."

"Maybe it's something everybody should experience," Oz says, but he doesn't believe it. The bartender brings more beer.

"Did I ever tell you about my last trip to Barrow?" Barney Barnett asks.

"No."

"People—my people—live in shacks made out of driftwood and sealskin, but they drive new snowmobiles down the tundra roads. Two-thousand-dollar snowmobiles."

Oz Crockett interrupts. "This is all old stuff to me. Don't you think I . . ."

"Shut up!" Barney Barnett shouts. "You've been wallowing in your own private existential ennui for fifteen years. At least my ennui isn't private. They only drive the snowmobiles a few times before they run them into embankments or the engine freezes or something. Then you know what happens? They take their welfare money and buy another and drive it until *it's* wrecked, too. There's nobody to fix the damn things so they just leave them where they break down. The tundra is littered with shiny new snowmobiles. Things don't rust in 30 below weather." Barney Barnett drinks half a bottle of Olympia in one tip. "That's why it's so inviting to take the last walk. Up there, wherever you fall is your home forever, and you'll never look a day older. Now do you know why I came back?"

Oz Crockett gets up from the table and stumbles away. There is no point in listening further. Barney Barnett is too drunk to make sense and Oz Crockett is too drunk to pay attention. As he leaves the bar, half a bottle of beer still clutched tightly in his hand, he looks back and sees Barney Barnett hollering for the bartender, holding a sheaf of greenbacks.

Oz Crockett slips on a patch of slush in the doorway and falls to his knees. That's all right: he needs to think anyway, and he thinks better sitting down. He crawls to the nearest wall and props himself up. A bloated Eskimo woman lumbers by pursued by a young roughneck down in his cups. It's a tough life.

Oz realizes that his father must have witnessed this blundering chase scene many times. It must have horrified him. The same sloughed-out, sluttish, slow-footed walk into some dreamed-up mountains. Some people find their courage in a bottle: others find mountains there. A whole culture was dying, why shouldn't he have been horrified? But Oz Crockett's father had wanted his ideals to live, so he left his cabin, his work, and his legacy to Oz. Well, well. A legacy of suicide. Better that, Oz supposes, than none. Oz feels a need to sleep right in the doorway. He feels his body grow heavy, almost limp. Then he hears voices.

"That dude—the fat skimo flashing a roll. He's our meat."

Oz Crockett looks up through slits and sees two townies, not much older than boys. They are dressed in denim and snow caps, and they are slouching.

"Quick, he's coming this way," whispers the other.

Oz Crockett moves his head and looks sideways at the two toughs. They are almost stepping on him. Was it possible that they didn't see him?

"I'll punch him in his fat stomach and you grab his wallet while he's bent over."

They're planning to mug someone in the bar. Oz Crockett turns his whole body around and sees Barney Barnett weaving toward the door. The two men are planning a crime not three feet away from a witness. It's insane. Then a thought strikes Oz Crockett that is even more insane. Who bothers with an old drunk? Who cares what an old drunk hears? Oz Crockett has turned invisible, and the Tippler has acquired another power.

No. Oz Crockett isn't the Tippler. The Tippler is a creation of fantasy and this is real life.

Oz Crockett struggles to his feet, but it's as if he's moving underwater. Still, the men pay him no mind. "Stop it!" he tries to shout, but his voice sounds far away in another dimension. He throws himself on one of the men, but is pushed away easily. The other man pulls out a thin knife and flashes it at him.

"Beat it, old timer, or I'll cut your guts out."

In slow motion, Oz Crockett swings out his arm and smashes the bottom of his beer bottle against the doorway. The crash nearly sobers him. Somehow, he has become the Tippler in mid-swing, and he grins as he slashes at the men with the jagged half of the bottle. The two men retreat a few steps into the doorway. The

Tippler has them bottled up.

"Who are you?" one of the men asks.

"Ozwald Crosscut," he replies.

Back in the bar, faces like fish faces stare at him with fish eyes as Barney Barnett's voice rains throughout the room. "Robbers!" he shouts. "They were going to take my money."

And the faces swim closer. For once they have something to fight against, and the drunken eyes turn grim. The two men try to take a step toward the door and the Tippler swings the bottle viciously. But it is still a heavy, slow motion swing, as if he has acquired the weight of an entire people. A whole sea of Eskimo faces advance like the shadow of a tidal wave, and the two men drown under the onslaught.

The Tippler strikes again, and so, b'god, does Oz Crockett.

Then, suddenly lightheaded, he passes out.

*   *   *   *   *

Oz Crockett wakes up to the sound of building. Someone must've carried him back to his cabin, undressed him, and put him to bed. The night before is still clear in his memory. His headache gives him superhearing, but the construction itself doesn't bother him. Everyone must kick and gouge away in trying to get what they want. But Oz Crockett's father had been wrong. There is hope. Regardless of who tries to take everything you have away, there is still a way to hang onto it.

As he dresses, Oz Crockett visualizes a political cartoon. There are four radically opposite political groups gathered back to back at the North Pole. All proceed to scurry as far away from each other as they can. Yet on the bottom of the earth, things look different, and when they meet there, they find they are all facing the same direction. In fact, they have been walking in the same direction all along.

Oz Crockett has traveled halfway around the world—far enough to know that he should stop before he begins heading backwards.

Is he happier in Alaska? It's hard to say. Here, at least, he has powers and abilities beyond those of other people. But to keep it up, he has to work at it daily. He runs a hand through his beard and sets out for the Malamute.

About the Author

P. V. LeForge was born in Detroit but has spent most of his life in Florida. He has been a mechanic, an editor, a gardener, a park director, and a semipro baseball player. He currently owns a bookstore in Tallahassee, Florida and is working on a novel.